Homicide
My Own

A novel by **Anne Argula**

D0012493

PLEASURE BOAT STUDIO

A Literary Press

Homicide My Own

By Anne Argula

Copyright © 2005

B+T 5/26/05 16L

Published by Pleasure Boat Studio: A Literary Press, 201 W.89th Street, #6F
New York, NY 10024 ,*Tel* 212.362.8563, *Fax* 888.810.5308
e-mail pleasboat@nyc.rr.com, *URL* www.pbstudio.com

Argula, Anne

First printing

Design and Composition by Francis P. Floro

Library of Congress Cataloging-in-Publication Data

Argula, Anne.
Homicide my own : a novel / by Anne Argula.
p. cm.
ISBN 1-929355-21-1 (alk. paper)
1. Police--Washington (State)--Fiction. 2. Indians of North
America--Fiction. 3. Fugitives from justice--Fiction. 4. Washington
(State)--Fiction. I. Title.

PS3601.R49H66   2005
813'.6--dc22   2004022424

"To my Guy"

1

Neither of these two cops had ever pulled that kind of duty before. One of them a man, the other a woman; one young and the other not so young; one dour and of few words, and the other more dour than he, but with a mouth when a mouth was needed. Why them?

The man was the young one, Odd Gunderson, and he hated living in Spokane, though he was born and raised there. He accepted the town of his father in the same way he accepted his father's politics, as a given until taken, or worn away; the same way he accepted his father's religion, an unsmiling Lutheranism. The woman was a transplant from the coal regions of Pennsylvania, via Los Angeles, where she had gone because of "Dragnet" reruns, and where she became a cop, and where she would still happily be a cop, cruising Hollywood Boulevard, if she hadn't married a pharmacist from Spokane.

Odd had ready enthusiasm for an impromptu road trip out of town. All he needed was his tapes, which consisted, the older one regrettably found out, of "Leaving-town-music" and "Rolling-into-town-music" and "Driving-in-the-lonely-night-music."

The older one, the woman, did not like music and had no tapes, nor any enthusiasm, for any trip at all. No method of transportation had yet been invented that could get this one willingly to that great place beyond city limits known as "Away." And she suffered hot flashes, searing uncurlings beneath the skin.

Odd saw the detail as a reward for something done well; the other one saw it as a punishment for something done wrong. The other one was named Quinn, and that would be me.

In those days I was sweating constantly. I was told it would pass. Like, when? I wondered. On that particular Thursday it showed no signs of abating anytime soon. That day, I was removing, in a professional manner, a nuisance from Denny's, a young man in a cheap suit who claimed to be running for President, nominated by Christ's acclamation. This was the sort of thing I did well, reasoning with the unreasonable, though I also acquited myself honorably whenever it was necessary to wrestle down a runner, to fire off some pepper spray, or to wield a baton. I had never had the occasion to draw my service automatic, and I hoped every day I never would.

Neither Odd nor I knew why we were so uncomfortable in Spokane. It was not a bad place to live. It wasn't Los Angeles, but even LA wasn't the place I had come to with big dreams. Not anymore. Spokane was okay. It was far enough away to escape the liberal influence of Seattle and establish its own identity. Unfortunately, that was as The Gateway to Idaho, a whole other kind of strangeness that included more rounds per minute, fired in a discriminate pattern, if you know what I mean. Swarthy folks were there few, and closely watched. Apple pickers from the Yakima Valley chose to strum their melancholy guitars on a Saturday night closer to their own bivouac. Even I, having never quite lost my Pennsylvania coal-cracker accent, was perceived as something disturbingly foreign, though I had lived there for twenty-five years, with a native son husband held in high regard.

I had two hours left on my watch after I had set the candidate off on a different campaign trail, when I got the call to come in. Odd was already there, at the lieutenant's desk. I looked at him, like, what's up, but he just shrugged.

"Charlie and Stacey's excellent adventure is over," the lieutenant said.

Charlie and who? I don't think Odd remembered either, though with him it's hard to tell. Unless something truly amuses him, at which time he cracks half a crooked smile, his face remains a blank.

"A security guy at an Indian casino on Shalish Island nabbed them," the lieutenant continued.

"Where's Shalish Island?" I asked, the first of a few questions I needed answered. Like, who's Charlie and Stacey and what do they have to do with me?

"Damn near in Canada."

On the wall map, the island looked a lot like a Chevy logo, slightly askew in relation to the mainland, as though the right side of the car, let's say an '80 El Camino, were up on the Canadian curb and the left side in the Bellingham mud. The island had no strategic position. From there you could go nowhere but back.

"I called Stacey's mother," said the lieutenant, "and she's on her own way right now. Charles, however, is our package."

It came back to me. Charles T. Houser, thirty, thirty-one, -two, a systems analyst with a degree in communications from Gonzaga, deep roots in the community, and no criminal record, jumped bail. He'd been busted for unlawful carnal knowledge, the complaint brought by his other girlfriend, the grown-up one. He was out long enough to pack a bag before he and his fourteen-year-old sweetheart Stacey took it on the arfy-darfy.

"You two have the honor of going to pick him up and bring him back here, without incident," said the lieutenant.

"Okay," said the Swede.

"Why us?" said I, not seeing the honor in it. Besides, I thought, why us? They had people for that sort of detail. Odd and I were ordinary in the extreme. Our folders held neither commendations nor reprimands. We were just day-to-day cops.

"Because I need my two best people on this," said the lieutenant. How could this be an insult? Trust me, it was. I'd tell you his name but who cares? He's a lieutenant, suspiciously thin, close set steely eyes, bristles for hair. He doesn't like me.

"They're holding him at tribal headquarters, at my request. The Indians would just as soon drop him down a white hole, but I talked to the chief, who seems like a stand-up guy. He'll keep him on ice for us. Only we've got to hustle. If we futz around, they'll have to turn him over to the county and it'll add another jurisdiction and another couple of levels of paperwork. Let's get him back to Spokane before anyone east of the reservation, like our own local newshounds or some young pussy protective society, finds out he's been had. It's a nice drive; you'll enjoy it."

Until you hit the Snoqualmie Pass, where you can run into snow in June and traffic at 120 mph, the drive from Spokane to Seattle is as boring a five hours' drive as God has ever devised, and then you still have to go north to this island I had never heard about before.

"I'll have to go home and change, shower," I said.

"What for? Shower when you get back."

Working with men all my life, I've grown tired of justifying hygiene. They sweat as much as we do, it just doesn't bother them.

"Besides," said the lieutenant, "I want you in uniform."

Rebuked, I argued for the new Lexus in the confiscated vehicle pool, but he gave us, as I knew he would, the shit-brown Chevy Lumina, with the cage in the back for restraining Charles T., the short-eyed lover boy.

"You stop for gas, for coffee, you stop to pee," the lieutenant said. "Let's say six and a half hours to get there. Here's your Xeroxed directions. Figure an hour for the transfer…"

Like that could happen. "More like two, my guess," I said.

"… Six and a half hours back."

"Overtime?" I asked. "Right?"

"Time off for time volunteered."

Da frick. Who volunteered? If he had asked for volunteers, I would have taken one step backwards… and never known.

2

Odd did not have to do anything before we left town, not pick up anything, or say anything to anyone. Me, I had to pull the shit-brown Lumina into the Rite-Aid lot on our way out of town and give Connors a kiss good-bye.

"Kiss Esther for me, while you're at it," he came up with.

I shot him a look.

"What?" All innocent.

"Kiss her yourself."

Esther worked behind the pharmacy counter with Connors and doled out the prescriptions he filled. Every man in town wanted to kiss her, and I thought most of them probably already had. If young men like Odd had lascivious thoughts about her, what about older men like Connors? The same thoughts squared. I worried about it because it had been nearly a year since I'd flatlined sexually. I was slowing down even before that.

I used to love it, but sex became a chore, one more wifely chore, and not the best of them. I'd rather iron, da frick.

To be fair, Connors had his husbandly duties too, and he came across without complaint. For example, I like to have dinner out at a nice place that doesn't have a salad bar. There are maybe three in Spokane. He'd rather eat at home, but he took me out once a week and he made it a pleasant thing for both of us. Why couldn't I make my obligation just as nice, bring a little imagination to it? At the time, it somehow never occurs to me. Every time we did it was a reminder of what I had lost so completely.

We were grown up; we always knew that over years life would change, and some of the change would happen in bed, but neither of us ever suspected that precious element of married life would disappear completely, never to be recovered. It was unfair. We knew in the grand scheme of things there were greater tragedies. Still, all I wanted was once and again to revisit where we used to be... but you can't get there from here.

At first, Connors thought it was him, that he had lost his appeal to me—what man wouldn't think that?—but I knew that no man would ever again light me up. I knew I was still attractive to men, they let you know, but it neither pleased me nor reassured me. Their long eyes meant nothing to me. It kind of pissed me off, to be truthful.

I stopped for a moment in the aisle, unseen, and watched Esther taking care of a customer. Connors was in the glassed-off pharmacy behind her, head down, doing his job. She was a beauty, how could you not notice, how could any man not imagine what it might be like, including my man. I used to have that. My calves, objectively speaking, are still every bit as good as hers, if maybe a little thicker, not that nice line of hard muscle that rose with her every step. I have her beat in the boobs too, only hers stand on their own. Once, I could have matched her in the doopa too, but twenty hours of delivering Nelson, along with twenty years of sitting in a squad car, had spread things out a little. What a wicked inventory!

It came down to the years, though, didn't it, the years that put her at one away from thirty and me only one shy of fifty. I had to believe that those years were to my advantage, because I had spent them all with Connors. That had to count for something.

Esther defined niceness. All of her conscious thoughts were directed to helping others in some way, preferably small but noticeable. She saw me and acted incredibly blessed for the experience, as though now at last her day was made. It made me want to puke. All I saw was an operator smart enough to flatter the wife of the man she'd like to steal. I feared that given the opportunity, he would jump it, so to speak. And why shouldn't he? How could I be so entirely uninterested in sex and at the same time so jealous he might enjoy it with someone else? Because that's the way I am. That's the way we all are.

I smiled at Esther the way you do at a bad joke, and caught Connors' eye. He came out and met me at the end of the counter. I explained the last-minute detail.

"That's the shits," he said.

"Tell me."

"The end of your watch, and they want you to…. And then turn around and come home and go to work the next day?"

"The green weenie," I agreed.

"Can't you get out of it?"

"Not without being an old lady about it."

Nobody wants to be an old lady. Connors understood that.

"Then let Odd do most of the driving."

"Okay."

"You ride in the back seat and try to get some sleep. You need your sleep."

"I will. I do."

"Why don't you just quit? The hell with it. We don't need the money."

"Twenty-two months and I'm outta there. Listen, I don't have anything at home for your dinner."

"Don't worry about it. I'll take care of myself."

He was a good husband. I had no complaints. I was the best wife I could be. He didn't complain either, though the silences were getting longer.

"See you in about... let's say, fifteen hours," I said.

He leaned over the counter and gave me a kiss.

All my life I have been aware, more than most people, of the possibility of sweeping changes during unexpected moments, and yet, like everyone else, I go on assuming things will occur more or less as they were supposed to occur. See you tomorrow, plumber on Tuesday, eight and a half percent interest, cloudy and mild, Woodlife the deck in August, early retirement in twenty-two more months.... What fools we are, ain't?

3

My old man had to take a yearly vacation. It was forced on him by my mother, who would not go along but believed it important for him to get away from the store once a year, for at least a week, though if he were to be gone for a week, the drive had better be three and a half days each way, because he never lasted longer than the drive itself. When I reached the age of sixteen and got my driver's license, I went with him.

He would sit next to me with a sixer of Bud, tune in the baseball game, and let me drive him all the way to Toronto or Atlanta or Rapid City, South Dakota. He had no love for those particular cities, no sights he wanted to see. Their only appeal was that they seemed far enough away to constitute a vacation, far enough away from Shenandoah, Pennsylvania, where we lived. The old man and I would reach Toronto or Atlanta or Rapid City, and we would stay the night in some eight-dollar motel. He would caution me not to walk around the room in my bare feet, because we did not know who occupied the room before us. We would have dinner, "supper," we called it, in some restaurant recommended by the desk clerk. Early the next morning, often before daybreak, we would start the long drive back to Pennsylvania, having seen nothing but the road, the motels, the restaurants. The old man could claim a vacation and my mother would leave him alone about it.

On the road, this is the story I told Odd, about me and my old man and our road trips. He got half a kick out of it, cracked half a smile.

"Were you a tomboy back then?"

"What makes you say that?"

"Relax. It's just the way I picture it."

"It was my transistion period. A year or two before, I played shortstop on the boys' team. I played center in vacant lot football, and it was only years later it dawned on me that I won that position so the guy playing quarterback could cop feels. I did some street fighting, too, and held my own."

"Your father still alive?"

"No, they're both gone."

"You had a good childhood, though, sounds like."

"Yeah, there was usually a lot of yelling but no one ever got hit. I was the only child, but nobody doted on me. Just the opposite. They made sure I was tough."

"There was never any yelling in my house," said Odd. "There was hardly any talking. I wasn't real sure I even belonged there."

"I had the same feeling! Felt out of place. In the family, in the town, da frick. Maybe it's that way with all kids."

"Could be. Like Spokane, I kept wondering why in the hell we had to live here, but nobody else seemed to think about it."

"How come you didn't just leave when you came of age?"

"Good question. It's not like I never thought about it."

"Still not too late. You'd qualify in most any other department."

"Yeah, but you'd miss me too much."

He was being sarcastic, but I would miss him if he left.

We burned the rest of the daylight getting to Ritzville. Once we stopped for gas and Odd offered to take over, but I wasn't feeling at all tired. Anyway, it was easier for me to drive than just to sit. We used the facilities at the gas station and he crawled into the back and fell right to sleep to one of his "driving-in-the-lonely-night" tapes.

He snored, softly at first, a comforting sound to me, really. It reminded me of Connors, when we used to sleep in the same bed, and of Nelson, when he lived at home and I would check on him. But as Odd's sleep deepened his snores became unsettled, harsh, jagged. A leg kicked out. Both of his arms shot out and folded over his head like a protective cowl, and then his breathing just stopped. I youkst the rearview mirror for a better look. Hell, he wasn't breathing. He was thirty-two,-three; how could he just stop breathing? I was about to pull to the side of the road and administer CPR when his lips puffed out with spent air and he started breathing again. "You never knew," he said in his sleep, as though talking over fences to someone two backyards away. "It's time."

I killed the music and drove on, keeping one eye on the road, one eye on him. He slept like that, repeating the pattern. I began to count slowly whenever he stopped breathing... one, two, three... nine, ten... fifteen, sixteen... and then a violent puff of air.

He went on like that until we made Moses Lake, where they interned the Japanese-Americans during World War Two.

"Odd? Odd? Odd?"

I kept calling his name, softly, until he awoke.

"Odd, do you know you do stuff in your sleep?"

"I do?"

"Big time. You kick out your legs and throw back your arms. Worst of all, you hold your breath. Woi Yesus, how does anybody sleep with you?"

As good-looking as he was, the question was rhetorical.

"I don't sleep too well."

"That's an understatement, if I just got a sample."

"Everybody's got something," he said.

"Ain't you tired during the day?"

"Sometimes. But my judgment's clear."

"No one said it wasn't. Don't get all defensive."

"I'm just saying I can do my job."

"I know that. But you could do with a medical check-up on the sleeping thing. You could pay for it yourself, so there's no insurance record."

"I'm fine. Don't worry about me."

"Okay, deal. You don't worry about me, neither."

"Why would I worry about you?"

"Just don't."

We hit a hatch of boonda bugs, which smeared the windshield opaque. The window washer couldn't keep up with it, so I pulled to the side and waited them out. To clean the windshield I had to sacrifice half a bottle of my Calistoga Springs water. I always have a bottle of water at my side because I need continual irrigation or I will spontaneously combust. I drank the other half, and we went to opposite sides of the road and watered the weeds.

No way was I going to turn over the wheel. By now I was tired, but at least I was awake. We got back into the car and motored on.

"You didn't have any 'Taking-a-piss-by-the-side-of-the-road-music'?" I said.

"I'll look for some."

We passed the long misery that lay between Moses Lake and Ellensburg in silence. I went into the right side of my brain, or is it the left? I'm never sure. Anyway, that side where whatever happens has no reason. I had some imaginary glimpses of Nelson aboard the USS *Abraham Lincoln*, standing inspection on the flight deck in his dress blues.

"This Houser guy, did he have a record?" Odd said, breaking the silence and my reverie.

"No. Just a victim of love, or something."

"Do you think he knew he was doing something wrong? I mean, do you think it bothered him?"

I thought he was legally sane, that was enough for me. Not for Odd.

"Wouldn't he know that in the end it would hurt them both, that it would end in pain and sorrowful stuff?"

A stiff prick has no conscience, I reminded him.

Rather than laugh, as most guys would, he only seemed to think more about it.

"It must be easy to fall in love with an underage girl; they're so sweet. But it must be very hard to find a safe way to express that love."

"Bullshit. You don't see grown women falling in love with underage boys."

"There was that teacher in Seattle."

"Looney tunes."

"Why couldn't I have had a teacher like that? Talk about learning something useful."

"That was strange in the extreme. And she's in prison for it, don't forget."

"Still, it happened. I think it happens a lot, but a real adult knows how to deal with it. A real adult knows how to sit and watch his impulses, watch them until they pass away, knows he don't have to be controlled by them. Like Houser was."

If I thought about it at all, I might agree, but on the subject of Charles T. Houser and Stacey all I could think about was they were the reason I was on this boring road instead of home in my own bed.

Maybe it was the night and the lonely road. I'd never heard Odd talk so much. I was already hoping it wouldn't carry over to the long return trip during which he might try to get into the prisoner's head, and I would have to say that we shouldn't talk to him without a lawyer in the car.

"What's Houser, thirty-two, thirty-three?" asked Odd.

Around that, as I recalled. Like Odd himself.

"A fourteen-year-old girl is impressed by the attentions of a man that age." He waited for me to confirm, and when I didn't, he said, "Isn't she?"

"Well, it's a new-found power. She's either scared or euphoric, but mostly she's embarrassed by the sheer inappropriateness of it."

"That's the way it was with you?"

"My father's friends, teachers, dentists... in a word, icky."

"Still, I think a lot of young girls are longing for someone to make them feel special."

I asked him how he knew so much about young girls, and he said it was only logical. "But no matter what happens," he said, "she's innocent. You can't blame her, no matter how enticing she was. The man is an adult; he's my age. He has a responsibility; he can't let anything happen, no matter how intense it gets or how natural it seems. He can't let it go too far."

Houser did, though, I pointed out. That's why we were here... but where were we? Nowhere yet. Washington prairie.

I knew Odd Gunderson pretty well, as well as you know a guy you work with and see every day. We buddied up a lot; I was drawn to him, in a non-sexual way. He was a good guy, and I liked him. At those times when you had to partner up, he would ask for me and I would ask for him. He was in the volleyball league, had great legs, was a ferocious spiker, a good competitor. He would have a beer with us after the game, some microbrew on tap, and sit quietly while the rest of us swapped war stories, but he'd cut out early and wind up later at The Box with that young civilian crowd, drinking cosmopolitans.

He was devoted to lawfulness, and that made him a good cop, but I always had the feeling he was not cut out for police work, and I never knew why he got into it. By the end of this detail, I would know. He couldn't be anything else. Before that, though, as I said, I saw an okay cop, a good volleyball spiker, one of the guys, with a life apart from the badge, a guy who maybe just examined things a bit deeper than the rest of us, those of us who were afraid to look too closely for fear of falling in, which in the end I did, holding onto Odd's sleeve, so to speak.

"What does he do to get this off him?" he asked.

What? Who?

"Houser, the grown-up. He's going to jail...."

Yes, and us taking him there.

"Will that do it? Will that remove the stain? Or does he, I don't know, have to do something? What would a person have to do to counterbalance letting his lust take him where it shouldn't go?"

I recalled at that moment that Odd was a Lutheran, which is not a faith known for its proselytizing but for its love of guilt. I was half-waiting for him to suggest that Charles T.'s only hope now was to accept Jesus as his personal savior and commence a meaningful relationship. But that was other guys on the force who were not a part of this. Every job has them, ain't?

For me there was nothing at all special about this case.

A yonko let his cock run away with his brains. Nothing unique in the annals of criminal offense. I told him all that in a few clipped and disinterested sentences. I'm sure I was a disappointment to Odd. He'd rather share this ride with one of the sequentially pierced and extensively tattooed, dazzlingly cropped white-haired girls from The Box, who could get into the causes and consequences of statutory rape and bring a lot more to the party. Charles T. Houser, to me, was no more than a day's work, an extra day's work.

Still, it was a long road and some conversation was required. I came back again to Odd's sleeping habits. I guess he could see I was honestly interested because he wound up telling me stuff he hadn't told God. As a child, he told me, he could sleep through the worst nor'wester. His sleep then was like a coma. Unhappily, he would not even wake up to pee. He was, he told me, a major bed-wetter up until about thirteen. His mother accepted it with gratitude that it wasn't anything worse, and just as she knew he would, he did eventually grow out of it. Then came the flailing of arms and legs, the talking, the walking. More recently, the night sweats and the insomnia. These last two we had in common, though I did not mention it.

All I said was, "You must want to die. Just for the sleep."

"What good is sleep if you never wake from it?"

If he expected an answer, he didn't get it from me.

4

Through the unexpected, if not happy, combination of injuries among their opponents and some equally unexpected, and certainly happy, flashes of professionalism and maturity on their own parts, the Seattle Sonics had made the playoffs and were in the NBA semi-finals. Quite an event, deserving of a new arena down the line. We hit some of that post-game traffic near the Space Needle and it slowed us down on I-5 all the way up to Lynnwood, where the Interstate freed up again and we cruised.

I kept it in the second lane at seventy miles per hour, more or less on autopilot by this time. Somewhere on that island I was going to have to find a place to nap before we turned around and did this all over again.

Fifteen miles south of Bellingham we started looking for the sign for the Shalish Ferry exit.

"It has to be around here pretty close, ain't?"

"Yeah, it's not far now," Odd said, and looked at his watch. "We should make the 12:45 ferry."

And there it was: "GOMEZ LANDING, SHALISH IS. FERRY, 1 MILE."

I eased off the gas, got into the exit lane, and left civilization. The way was marked and in ten minutes the two-lane country road took us to a one-lightbulb landing and an eight-car ferry left over from the mosquito fleet days and of questionable seaworthiness. I paid our fare, tucked the receipt behind the visor, and rolled aboard, the sixth car on, and nobody behind us. A few walkaboards came out of nowhere and huddled on deck, exposed to the weather, which tonight was just a little chilly. Everybody else stayed in his car.

I put my head against the window and went right out.

Fifteen minutes later. Odd woke me up by gently rubbing my arm. It felt nice. "Wake up, Quinn," he whispered.

I awoke and heard motors starting up.

"We know where we're going?"

"I don't think we can get too far lost," he said. "It's an island; you'll run into water eventually."

We left the ferry and fell into the slow pace of a crawling caravan of six cars.

"How did you know there was a 12:45 ferry?" I asked.

"Huh?"

"Back on the Interstate... you said, we should make the 12:45. Was that written down?"

"You got the paperwork."

"I didn't see that written down."

"What did I say?"

"That we could catch the 12:45 ferry."

"The lieutenant must have said so."

"I didn't hear him say that, what time the ferry left."

"I don't know, it just came into my head, I guess."

There was more than the one road on the island, we discovered, as the other cars from the ferry turned off and disappeared into the tall firs and cedars. We stayed on what we thought was the main road until it made a sweeping right turn and there, in the still dark night where America blended into Canada, sat an Indian's vision of a bit of Las Vegas.

A free-standing marquee, large and imposing, in front of a series of three Quonset huts bolted together, promised more than the place could possibly deliver. Lavish buffets at giveaway prices, liberal card-operated slots, a rock-and-roll group from the sixties that I knew for a fact had long ago lost three of its four to the natural failing of internal organs. On either side of the curve in the road, both sides of the casino, was a scattering of crosses marking the demise of drivers who had been in too great a hurry either to get to or to leave the place.

"Here's where Charlie got busted."

"We should stop," said Odd.

"Why?"

"See how it went down."

"How it went down?"

"Yeah, Charles and Stacey."

"What do we care how it went down?"

It felt silly, talking like that, how things went down.

Odd said, "Duh? We're cops."

"The cop stuff has already been done. We're pick-up and delivery."

By that time we had passed the casino.

"We could eat," he said. "It said buffet."

That did it, of course. There has never been a cop who could resist a cheap smorgie. I turned around and pulled into the lot, which was near full, out there in the middle of the night, middle of nowhere.

Sometimes you forget you're in the uniform and you walk around like an ordinary person. We strolled in, and every head turned from the dice or the cards to see us standing at the entrance. It was a small place and shabby, and the people in it looked sad and lost.

A boonda guy with a face like this side of the moon and wearing a powder blue blazer came up to us, walking with a limp. His name tag said KING GEORGE. It might have been last name first. He could have been George King. But I didn't ask. I didn't call him anything.

"You from Spokane?"

We said we were.

"We don't have 'em here. They're over at the Tribal Police Station."

"Yeah, well, we wanted to check out where it went down," I said.

He looked at me the way I had looked at Odd, who was looking at me that way right now. How it all went down.

"Where they were busted. And, besides, we're hungry. We've been on the road all day and missed supper."

So the security guy with the moon face led us to the eats and told the cashier we were compted and handed us each a large oval plate, which was a good sign because my theory is that everything tastes better on an oval plate. Short ribs and noodles, fried chicken, taco makings, squares of cake—nothing fancy but plenty of it. We took our chow to one of the small square formica tables. Low rent all the way.

"I was the one busted 'em," said the boonda security guy.

"Well... congratulations." I could care less. He told us
all about it anyway.

He had been watching them from the minute they came
in the door. Together, they didn't look right. The legal age
was eighteen and it was unlikely the girl was that old. The
man was way older.

How the fugitive lovers found their way to Shalish
Island and this funky casino was never fully explained,
not that I cared. This was only one of many little casinos
dotting Northwest Indian Territory and far from the most
inviting. Besides, it was difficult to find, considering the
ferry ride. I thought they were surely not looking for a
casino, but an island, which has universal appeal both to
lovers and harried fugitives. Still, it was the casino they
found, and in which they themselves were found, by the
boonda security guy sitting with us while we chowed.

When Houser and his little biscuit went through the
buffet line, King George got a cup of coffee and sat nearby
to eavesdrop on their conversation, but for a long time there
was no conversation. They joined hands across the table
and, heads bowed, offered a long silent grace. King George
said he wondered were they listing the items on their plates
in alphabetical order or were they taking the opportunity to
be grateful for other things as well. As though on cue, he
said, their heads rose simultaneously and they dug in.

"I should, you know, call," said Stacey.

"Not a good idea," said Charles.

"Just to let her know everything's okay."

"You think everything's okay?"

"You know…."

"It is okay. Everything is fine. We're together. I'll take care of you."

"I love you so much."

"I love you too, Stacey. I'm crazy for you, like literally. I'm insane."

"Me too! I'm out of my mind."

"There's no turning back now."

They held hands again, but with the free hand they kept on feeding. They were in love, but it had been some time since they'd last eaten.

"I'm going to have to get a job somewhere," said Charles.

"I can get a job, too."

"What doing?"

"Anything. At a MacDonald's, or in a store or something. Let's go to Hawaii!"

"All right."

"Really?"

"Whatever you want, Sweetie. Only first, we have to get jobs and save enough to get there."

"We can put it on your credit card."

"I can't use that anymore. They can trace you through your credit card, map your whereabouts day by day."

King George by then had heard quite enough to get the picture and to wonder what role he and his tribe should play, if any, in this little drama. His options? He could finish his coffee, go about his business, and keep one eye on them until they left, which he assumed would be shortly after they had eaten all they could hold. If something unfolded afterwards, however, something untoward—if he killed her or she killed him, or if they held up the cafe or mugged an old Indian, or maybe killed themselves in a lovers' suicide pact, which was not all that remote an idea since their conversation had turned to the eventual movie of their lives and who should play each of them in the major production, which she decided ought to be Leonardo DiCaprio and Drew Barrymore and he countered with the argument that he was too young and she was too old, Leonardo and Drew, that is—if anything like that happened and it was later revealed they had spent some time in the casino, it would all come back to what was an underaged girl doing in a tribal casino and where was security? Or he could go over there and invite them both to follow him to the room where they talk to people, away from the action, which always runs the risk of a public relations *faux pas*, embarrassing but not really all that dangerous since you can't sue Indians.

For the moment, King George just nursed his coffee and listened in on what the couple imagined might be the true happy ending to their scenario.

"We could get married," mused Charles.

The young girl leapt to her feet, danced around the table, and planted a kiss on his lips.

Some midnight snackers looked up from their macaroni and meat sauce, thinking some lucky bastard had hit a Keno combo.

"Yes! Yes! Yes!" she trilled, though to King George's ears it had sounded like something less than an actual proposal of marriage. Charles smiled, entertained by her youthful enthusiasm, as was King George, in his way, but he never smiled. Stoicism was his birthright.

"We could leave the country," she said, still on her feet, "we could get married in Hawaii. That'd prove to everybody we were seriously in love; that would show the whole world the power of love over cops."

"It's a thought," said Houser.

"Yes, yes, yes!" she accepted for the sixth time.

"If we even could get legally married..." Charles mused.

"If? Why can't we? Legally married? Can't we?"

"Maybe. For sure we'd need your mother's permission, though. Hawaii's, you know, a state."

"Shit.... There's always something shooting down a cool idea. Wait. You know what? She might go for it. She might be glad to get rid of me. She always calls me a real handful. She gets all drama queeny and goes, 'You are the revenge of my own youth.' She might be thrilled to have you take me off her hands!"

He talked to her in a soft and loving way, trying to calm her down. "Things have to cool down a bit, Honey, before we can bring up that subject with your mother. We have to get her on our side after everything cools to a simmer."

King George made up his mind that some action was necessary. Casino security, indeed, the tribal police, had long suffered disrespect from the sheriff's department and the white population of the island. Though sovereign, the tribal efforts at law enforcement, especially as it applied to non-tribal members, were for the most part ignored. Traffic tickets, for example, were routinely torn up and scattered in the wind. It was embarrassing.

King George was surprised that when they finished their food, the lovers went in two different directions. He chose to follow the girl to the bank of three public phones where she placed a collect call. King George picked up one of the other phones, turned his back to her, and listened.

"Hi, Mom, how're you? Look, I'm okay, okay? I'm with a friend, okay? No, a girlfriend... you don't know her, okay? I have lots of friends you don't know. Nancy, all right? Her name is fucking Nancy, and we're in California, okay? I'm not sure... between San Francisco and Los Angeles."

Seems she got busted on that because the operator must have told the mother where the call was coming from. There was a little bit of controlled screaming, from both ends of the line. The girl turned it back on her mother, blaming her for always making her lie. There was hissing and half-said rebuttals and counter-accusations before the mother said something that stopped the daughter and changed her tone of voice. "They are? The cops? It's none of their business! I don't know where he is, okay? I thought he was back there. Tell the cops I'm all right and I don't know where he is, okay? How do you know? You think you know everything. All right, all right, yeah, we're together, but nobody is ever gonna separate us. Mom?

Listen, Mom? You ought to give us permission to get married."

Apparently the mother thought that was a terrible idea, because the girl kept repeating the words "Why not?" with growing intensity until she split them with the word "fucking."

King George hung up his phone and walked slowly toward the man, who was at the craps table, and, coincidentally, winning. He paused halfway there and spoke into his walkie-talkie. "Sidney? King. Craps table. The man with the dice. He's with an under-aged girl. Get Bobby, just in case."

The girl slammed down the phone and went to the craps table.

King George took his time, then stood behind the croupier for a moment.

The girl squeezed in next to the man and draped an arm over his shoulder. The man said, "I'm winning, sweetie! Blow on these puppies." She blew on the dice and he tossed them. Seven, a winner.

"I asked my mom. She went ballistic."

"Huh?"

"About getting married and stuff."

"Stacey, didn't I tell you…?"

"I think maybe we'd better go to Canada or somewhere. That's a different country, right? We can do stuff there we can't do here, right?"

King George nodded to Sidney Everybodytalksabout, who approached the table, and to Bobby Young Elk, who was drawing toward them. Before Charles could make another pass, King George asked him to hold up. "Is this young lady with you?"

Charles and Stacey looked at each other. She quickly withdrew her arm. "No," they said simultaneously.

"I know that's a lie, so I'll ask another question. Young lady, are you eighteen?"

"Eighteen? I wish," said Stacey. "I'm twenty-two."

"Please pick up your chips and leave the floor with me."

The thrill of the gamble, what thrill there is in watching your money raked away, was put on hold as everyone observed the unfolding of this encounter. Charles, in no rush, gathered up his chips in two handfuls.

"Where're we going?" he asked, in a pleasant, unconcerned voice.

"We'd like to talk to you, maybe make a phone call."

Stacey brought her foot down hard on King George's instep, and though she weighed only 98 pounds with a Discman hanging around her neck, he felt every ounce of it. They ran for the door, where Sidney Everybodytalksabout swept up Stacey in a bear hug, her feet kicking in the air.

Charles had already dropped most of the chips in his left hand. What he had in his right hand, he threw into Bobby Young Elk's face.

He was on his way to the rear entrance with a good lead.

He made the parking lot. He would have made the car, might have even made the ferry, had a sherbet's chance in hell of making the mainland, no chance in hell of living happily ever after.

He dropped his last few chips into the shirt pocket of the valet parking attendant and waited to be put in handcuffs.

Odd and I ate up, all the while listening to the story, and then we went off to pick up Houser.

5

The Tribal Police Headquarters was a double-wide trailer behind a B.P. station, closed for the night. It was 2:00 a.m. by the time we found it. We had already burned the hour the lieutenant had allotted us for the pick-up. I knew that would happen, but what's another hour on a detail like this?

The young Indian behind the desk had the dull embarrassed patina of the lowest dangling link on the chain of command.

I gave him the paperwork the lieutenant had given us.

"We're here to get Charles Houser."

He studied the paperwork earnestly. He was about eighteen.

"I have to call the chief," he said.

"The Indian chief?"

"The chief of police," he said. I knew that with the best intentions, and I'm not claiming those were the kind I always had, I was helpless to keep from making offensive remarks. I was actually surprised it had taken so long.

The kid picked up the phone, dialed and said, "There's cops from Spokane here." He listened for a beat, then handed the phone to me. "He wants to talk to you."

"Quinn speaking."

"They sent a woman?"

"The name is Officer Quinn. Good morning."

"Seth Shining Pony. I'm head of the police here. I called Spokane, but unfortunately you had already left."

"I don't like the sound of this, Chief. This is sounding like a problem."

"A small problem, yes."

"Let me have it."

"You won't be able to take the man back with you, at least not tonight."

"Why not?"

"I'll be right down. Tell Robert to make you coffee."

He hung up before I could say anything more. I gave the phone back to Robert and turned to Odd. "There's a problem."

"Sure there is. There always is."

"He's on his way to fill us in. Hey, Robert, you wouldn't happen to know, would you? What the problem is?"

Robert was like every nurse in every hospital I've ever been in. She knows the whole scoop, but the doctor will have to talk to you about that.

I sat on a tattered easy chair they had there. This place was unlike any police headquarters I had ever seen. Nothing to read, nothing to do, so I just sat there, much like Odd suggested a sensible adult ought to do, watching one's impulses until they faded away. In my case, I wouldn't mind some kind of impulse falling upon me so that I could let it take me wherever the hell it was going. Impulses can be good things too.

Odd was going over the bulletin board, your basic notices of what's happening in the jurisdiction and who's on the arfy-darfy.

A corner of a faded photograph, a five-by-seven, showed

beneath a sheet of thermal fax paper. Odd lifted the paper to see the photo in its entirety; then, like he owned the place, he reposted the fax somewhere else on the board, letting the light shine on a photo of a couple, a teenage couple, whose names were printed below the photo, but from where I sat I couldn't read them, if I cared, which I didn't.

Odd, though, couldn't take his eyes off the thing.

"Who are those people?" I asked. And when Odd didn't answer, I said, "Robert?"

"Huh?"

"That picture, who are those people?"

Robert looked up from his *Street Rods* magazine and over at the object of Odd's fascination. "That's Jimmy Coyote and his girlfriend, Jeannie Olson."

"They're dead," said Odd, sadly, which I suppose was not a great feat of detection, considering where we were, and the picture was so old.

"Yeah, long time past," said Robert. "Shotgunned, both of them, off at Point Despair in Jimmy's pick-up truck. It was a Ford."

"Who did that?" I asked.

"They never caught the killer," said Odd, transfixed before the photo of the young doomed couple.

"Nope. That's why their picture is still up there. Oldest unsolved crime on the island. The only murder unsolved."

"You have lots of murder out here?" I asked.

"Oh, yeah. Mostly from drunk fights or domestic squabbles, though. Jimmie 'n Jeannie was the last real murder."

"C'mere and have a look, Quinn."

"That's all right." I didn't need to have a look.

"She was a real heartbreaker."

"The old-timers say she was the most beautiful girl on the island," Robert said. "Most beautiful girl there ever was on the island. That's what they all say."

"No good suspects?" I asked.

"Lots of suspects. Nearly a thousand. Everybody who lived on the island. Only they could never figure out which one done it. Check it out, I have the only iron-clad alibi."

"You weren't born yet."

"Right."

Odd continued to stare at the photo. He was into it. Everybody loves a mystery, right? Wrong. I don't love a mystery. People get killed, other people either get caught for it or get away with it.

"Quinn, when were you born?"

"Why?"

"Can't you ever answer a simple question?"

"One-eleven. Okay?"

"What year?"

"None of your business."

"This girl was born on January 11… 1951."

My birthday. Did I make anything out of this? I put my head back and fell asleep, that's what I made out of it. It is a statistical fact that at any random gathering of twelve people, two of them will be found to have the same birthday. I don't know how that can be, but they say it is. Coincidences in life abound. People accept them.

The chief took his own sweet time. I had most of an hour's nap before Odd woke me saying, "This must be him."

"That's him," said Robert.

Chief Shining Pony was a serious man in his mid-forties, putting on a little weight. His long black hair, tied in two braids, was already turning silver at the temples. He was not in uniform. He wore jeans and cowboy boots and a fringed leather jacket over an Ex-Officio shirt. He led us into his tiny office in a corner of the back half of the double-wide and asked us to sit down.

"Did you lose him?" I asked, right out, which apparently was strike two on me.

"No, ma'am, we didn't lose him."

"Then what's the problem?"

"He tried to commit suicide."

"Aw, shit. How close did he get?"

"Not very. If you open up that door...."

Odd opened the door he indicated and we saw a ratty cell, just a cot, no sink or toilet, with the cell door now swung open. Blood all over the floor.

"That door was open, and I was here," said Seth Shining Pony, "so I caught him at it before he could finish. But if he was only makin' a gesture, it was one fine dramatic gesture."

"How so?"

"He tried to chew open a vein in his wrist."

"Woi Yesus."

"That's how he was going to remove the stain," said Odd.

"With his own teeth."

"What stain?" asked the chief.

"Of his actions."

"We're no strangers to suicide around here," said the chief. "I've seen Drano drinkers and plastic bag heads, but your boy takes the cake."

"Where is he now?"

"Laid up in bed, in my house. Some might say we should have ferried him or airlifted him to the hospital in Bellingham, and some might say we shouldn't have had him here in the first place. I was doing your boss a favor, and we did, after all, make the arrest. If I have to, I can debate it. But I'm hoping I won't have to. I'm hoping you two can carry him home tomorrow and, when the time is right, give us a little credit for a job well done."

"Fine by me, but what kind of shape is he in?"

"He didn't lose all that much blood. It's an ugly-ass wound but it's superficial. Problem is, now he's got a fever, chills, and the shakes. I'm guessing he might have poisoned himself with his own bite."

"When are we gonna know?"

"By tomorrow. If he did poison himself, then the cat is pretty much out of the bag and I'll have to turn him over to the sheriff."

"I better call Spokane."

"Like I told you, I already did. Your lieutenant says to spend the night and bring him back tomorrow."

"Did he say where we're supposed to sleep?"

"You can have the cell there."

I took another look at the blood splatters. "I don't think so."

"There's the davenport in here," said the chief.

Child rapist gets the spare bedroom, cop gets the flea-bitten davvy.

"And Odd?"

"What's odd?"

"I'm Odd," he said. "It's a Scandinavian name."

"Sorry. Does sound a little funny, though."

"Not like Shining Pony," I put in.

"I can sleep in the car," Odd said, "but I'm not tired. In fact, if you're up, Chief, I wouldn't mind talking to you."

"Leave it," I said, and I realized how bad it sounded. It is, after all, a recommended command in training your dog to avoid distractions. But I was pissed off and exhausted and I didn't want to take on any more than we had, which was already enough to get us into trouble.

"Go to sleep, Quinn. I'm on my own time here."

"Just stay out of what don't concern us, is all I'm saying."

"I don't mind talking," said the chief. "I'll just get a blanket and a pillow for your boss here."

I think that Indian was rubbing it in. "I'm not his boss," I said, before Odd could. "We're partners."

He gave me a blanket and pillow, nothing you'd want to put on your own bed, but in a pinch would be willing to use for a few hours on a borrowed davvy. They went outside together.

6

I slept for about four hours and could have slept longer but for the smell of the coffee Odd was holding under my nose. I pulled my legs off the davvy and took the coffee.

"You don't look the worse for wear," I said. In fact, he looked rested, bright, and clear-eyed. I didn't know whether he found a way of shaving or just didn't need to every day. He was fair and his beard was soft and light. Anyway, he didn't look like a man who had been on the road and up all night.

"What have you been up to?"

"Talking to the chief."

"That guy hates me."

"He didn't say. I went with him up to the crime scene."

"There's been a crime?"

"Their old murder case. It happened at a lover's lane. Two shots, out of a shotgun. Two kids. That's where we were, up there, me and the chief."

"In the middle of the night? When you could have been sleeping?"

"I was curious."

"You see, I'm not. It was long ago, in another place."

"It was in this place."

"Long ago."

"And nobody knows what happened."

"So you're at the scene of the crime, you and Chief Shining Pony."

"The hairs stood up on the back of my neck. I got a little dizzy."

"We all get dizzy. It passes."

"The place was spooky, I'm saying."

"It was late at night. The wind was blowing."

"No, it wasn't."

"So what was so spooky?"

"A feeling... a sense in the air. There wasn't much to see, but you could feel it, that something terrible had happened there."

"Would you have felt it if nobody had told you somebody was murdered there?"

"How the hell do I know? All I know is I felt it then. I walked around with the chief and you could feel it in the air. Quinn, I have an idea why those two kids were killed."

"Oh, yeah? I think I do too." I pressed my finger to my temple, as though I were the swami, conjuring hard. "The Mighty Quinn says... one of them was an Indian, and one of them was white, and that's why they were murdered."

"Right! Absolutely right! That's exactly what I was thinking."

The kid was adorable. You could say he was animated, but anyone who knew Odd wouldn't believe you.

"I think they've probably figured that much out for themselves," I said. "The racial thing."

"Yeah, maybe, but the whole case was so badly managed. The night was rainy, no good for prints in the mud, and no spent shells on the ground, but from the sound of it they didn't do much with the vehicle or even go after the racial end of it. This thing's been on my mind all night."

"Then it's time to think of something else. Like why we are here. Like our prisoner. What's the word on him?"

"We're supposed to go over there, to the chief's house. We've been promised breakfast."

"Very nice. I'd rather be promised the prisoner. Why do I have this growing sense of dread, like things are going to go, oh, so wrong and someone's gonna have to be blamed and a turd will find its way into my folder?"

"Eat a banana. You're probably low on potassium."

Low on estrogen, more like it. As cool and as crisp as Odd looked, that's how hot and sticky I felt. I wanted to rip off my shirt. I'm sure I was smelling ripe. I went into their little bathroom and took a standing bath with wet paper towels. All I had was lipstick, so I did my lips and let the rest go to hell.

Odd talked to me through the closed door.

"Seventy percent of this island is tribal land, all but the northeastern part, which is unincorporated county, with a sheriff's station."

That would be the top part of the Chevy logo that the island looked like on the map.

"The tribe runs the ferry and the casino and six weeks out of the year, right now, as a matter of fact, they can sell fireworks. They also sell cigarettes, tax-free, but they're supposed to be smoked on Indian land. Right. The school, K through 12, is on the white part of the island, but kids have been going there for generations, white and Indian, without any problems."

"Is this a tour? Are we on vacation here?"

"It's an interesting place, Quinn. They never had any real problem before so they couldn't accept it might have been racial."

"This is what you've been doing, all night long, instead of sleeping?"

"Now, you'd never know it, 'cause Indian kids and white kids pair off all the time and nobody thinks anything of it, but back then it was different. The sixties came and old restrictions were being tested."

"Odd, listen to me, you ain't a detective. You're a cop, and not even a cop from around here. We issue citations, we quell domestic disputes, we roust hookers and dope smokers, and we are sent on shit details like this that no one else wants."

"I know that."

I had to laugh. I packed the twins into my sports bra, put on my shirt and buttoned it up. I put on my pistol belt and shook it into the familiar fit on my hips, noticing lately how the rig seemed to be getting heavier.

I opened the door, took the last sip of coffee and handed him the empty cup.

"So it's off to evaluate our prisoner?" I said.

"Right. At the chief's house."

"You got the directions?"

"Sure." He looked at me, his lower lip jutting out ever so slightly, like an irresistible little boy.

"But it's right on the way and would only take a minute and what's the harm," I said, pretending to be him.

"What's that?"

"The scene of the crime."

This time, I got a full-tilt smile out of him.

"I got a feeling, Quinn. A very strong feeling."

"You could just sit quiet until it goes away," I said.

"I tried that," said he.

He drove. The road was lined with fireworks stands, put together with plywood and scrap lumber, with hinged wooden shut-downs over counters packed high with brightly wrapped pyrotechnics from China. Hand-lettered signs identified each stand. They seemed to be family enterprises. We later learned that the teen-aged son of each family was obliged to sleep in the shuttered stand with a .357 magnum tucked under his pillow to protect the investment from vandals and thieves. According to law, the fireworks purchased on the reservation must be set off on the reservation, but of course mainlanders came over and filled up their trunks, turning their own quiet neighborhoods into war zones, terrifying the family pets and invariably blowing off some of the little digits of their own children. Don't get me started on fireworks. More distractions for the dumb. Fireworks have killed and maimed more people than marijuana, which to date hovers around zero, but one is legal and encouraged, the other one can get you hard time. Don't get me started.

Odd pulled to the side of the road. A narrow rutted dirt road went up a hill and disappeared into the woods. "We have to walk from here," he said.

"You didn't say anything about walking."

Having come this far, I knew it would be a waste of breath to refuse, and I was going to need all the breath I had for the hike. We trudged up the hill.

"James Coyote had a Ford four-by pickup with a canopy. They had no trouble getting up here, even though it was raining that night and the road was all muddy. Lots of kids used to run their four-by's up here during the daylight, and at night it was a good place to bring a girl."

"You came up here last night with the chief?"

"Yeah, I told you. He's an interesting guy. That picture on the bulletin board, all these years, even though it's a cold case? He was only twelve when it happened. He knows there's a killer going free, maybe still on this island, and it still eats at him."

"And at you, apparently."

"It's got to me. I admit it. When we walked up to this rise last night, the chief and me, I started getting all roiling inside."

"I know what that's like."

The road rose into the woods and dropped into a clearing that over the years had been worn into a kind of four-by track, up and down hillocks, dangerous angles and curves, deep mud traps. Where it went up it offered a nice view of the water, Point Despair, one of the many cheerfully named points of land in the Northwest. Point Deception, Point No Point, Point Doom....

"This is where they parked," he said, showing me a lane that ended just inside the edge of the woods. "Jimmy backed in so that they were facing the water, even though there wasn't much to see that night because of the rain. They were alone, off in their own world, necking, touching each other, talking about their dreams."

"Did they have the radio on?" I was making a lame joke, adding one more impossible-to-know detail to his imaginary scene.

"No," he answered. "The radio was broken when Jimmy bought the truck and he never had the money to replace it."

"How do you know that?"

"The chief told me."

"Did he tell you they were talking about their dreams?"

"How could he know that?"

"How could you, buddy?"

"Isn't that what any young couple would talk about?"

"You were up here all night?"

"Half the night. There wasn't that much left to it."

"With Chief Shining Pony?"

"He's haunted. Comes here often. And he was only twelve when it happened. He kind of liked having the company and someone to talk to about it. You aren't interested?"

"Murder is always a little interesting, Odd, 'cause we're the only animals that practice it and study it... and seem to enjoy it. That's the mystery to me, not who did what to who."

"Is it because we're made in God's image? Do we get it from Him?"

"Hmmm…. Man's disposition toward murder is genetic, passed down from his Heavenly Father. That'll get you kicked out of any Lutheran church in the land, Odd."

He was standing where the driver's window might have been that night.

"They were shot from here," he said, "twelve gauge shotgun. First Jimmy, one shot to the head."

"The chief told you that? That the boy was shot first?"

"There were bruises on his right arm, where Jeannie had clutched him while they talked to the killer."

"They talked to the killer?"

"The window was rolled down. Why would the window be rolled down? It was pouring rain. Unless they rolled it down to talk to the killer? Which doesn't necessarily mean they knew him. They were polite kids. Still, with a population of only a thousand, odds are they did know him. Anyway, it wasn't a friendly conversation. She was gripping his arm. The killer shot Jimmy… then… Jeannie… then… he picked up the spent shells. Which is cold… methodical. Who could be so cold?"

Odd's eyes were focused on the interior of that imaginary Ford four-by, but mine were all over him, watching him play this out. I had never attributed a great imagination to Odd, but why would I? He was like me. He did his job, he went home.

"Over in that direction lives—or used to live, he's dead now—an old bachelor strawberry farmer. You can't drive there from here, the only access is by another dirt road off the main road. His house is about half a mile hike from here. For a long time he was the prime suspect. He had complained about the kids and the noise they made over here and the way they tore up the land, even though it was county land... did I mention that? We're on white land here. If they had been killed on tribal land, the FBI would have had jurisdiction, and probably a much better chance of solving it. But the case went to the Sheriff's Department, and they didn't know murder from mahogany. They fixed on that strawberry farmer, who had lived alone for years and had turned eccentric. They didn't look anywhere else. They all thought that either he was here when the kids arrived or wandered by them when they were parked, and his anger at kids in general overtook him and...."

"Wandered by? Carrying a shotgun? In the rain and the mud and the dark, half a mile from his warm and cozy home?"

"Welcome to the case, Quinn."

"Fuck you, Odd. Let's get breakfast."

"I had no idea what you were like before breakfast."

"Now you do."

7

I wanted nothing more than for Charles T. Houser to be in the pink and homesick for Spokane. Odd was beginning to pose a danger to my own fragile equilibrium, because under normal circumstances I was a boo away from collapsing into tears. I could not tolerate behavior that was obsessive, compulsive, impulsive, passionate or inappropriately light-hearted; none of that nor sad country songs. I could not stand for things to take an unexpected turn, and me without a plan.

A light rain started to fall, sun filtering through, so that you could almost count the drops. I daydreamed running naked through those cool delicious raindrops.

Odd turned off the main road and up a gravel driveway to the chief's house. For a moment, it felt as if we were back in Spokane called to quell a domestic disturbance because on the porch was the chief himself, being yelled at and obscenely gestured to by an hysterical young girl, while a middle-aged woman sat defeated on the step, holding her head as though someone had hit her upside same. And as often happened back in Spokane, the disturbance back-pedalled upon the appearance of two uniformed officers getting out of a car.

"Morning, Chief," said Odd.

"Let me guess," said I. "This has to be little Stacey and her mother...."

"Gwen," the mother introduced herself.

Stacey took a moment to check our patches, then spit out, "You have no jurisdiction here. Fuck off!"

"She's been informing me of her rights," said the chief. "She seems to know a lot about that."

"I have a right to see him, goddammit! I have to know he's okay!"

"I told you, this is not a public place. This is my house and you're not going inside."

"Are you okay?" I asked the mother.

She rolled her eyes, as though wanting a definition of okay.

"Look, take your daughter home.... You're driving?"

"Yeah, that's our car," said Gwen, pointing to a half-primered Civic in the driveway.

"Take her home and have a long talk... about the birds and the bees. Long overdue, looks like."

"Fuck you, you old cunt!"

"Stacey!" admonished her mother, to no effect, then explained to us, "She wasn't raised to talk like that."

"Listen, young lady," I said, "this is Indian land, and this man is the law here. They don't have to indulge you; they can just throw you in jail."

"Go for it, you fat fucker!"

So much for idle threats.

I asked to see the prisoner and the chief invited us inside.

"If they can see him, I can see him too!" yelled Stacey, and she made the mistake of grabbing my arm as I was going inside the house. I hit her with the pepper spray, a good blast right in the face. She reeled back and screamed so loud I expected glass to break, which would have been some small satisfaction if it had been the pain of her taking her medicine, but it was more of her bottomless anger. She made choked and snotty threats to file the largest lawsuit we had ever seen. Fourteen years old.

Charles T. Houser was kept in the locked guest room, though at the moment the lock seemed unnecessary. He was ashen white, only half-awake, and if he was hearing the shrill voice of his own true love downstairs on the porch, as we certainly were, it seemed to have no restorative benefits.

He was on a high rough-hewn bed of cedar, covered against the morning chill with a handmade quilt of a bear design. He had been nursed by the chief's wife, a pleasantly plump woman with braided hair who might have been a beauty in her youth. So might have we all.

His arms were above the quilt and the right wrist, where he had attempted to gnaw his way to redemption, was heavily bandaged. His eyes fluttered when he saw us come to his bedside, as though he needed any more proof of the seriousness of his situation. I looked at him for a moment, felt no need for introductions, but thought I'd better recite him his rights first off, which I did, while the others held their places respectfully, as though it were some kind of prayer. He was under arrest. Again.

"How is he?" I asked Mrs. Shining Pony.

"He'll live," she said, without sympathy. It's hard to find sympathy among middle-aged women for a man who will seduce a fourteen-year-old girl.

"Mr. Houser," I said, "we're here to take you back to Spokane."

He looked from one to the other of us with frightened eyes, then raised himself slightly, his head moving back and forth as though looking for something.

Mrs. Shining Pony grabbed a bucket off the floor next to the bed and held it under his mouth. Into it he spewed a great rush of fluids, gagged, and did it again, before falling back to the pillow. He was spent, and oblivious to the cries from below, "Charlie! Charlie! I love you, Charlie!"

I took a look into the bucket, to check for blood, but it was nothing more than breakfast.

"I'm going to have to call Spokane," I said.

I did that while Odd sat down with the chief and his wife for the breakfast we were promised. I took a cup of coffee with me, in case it was going to be a call of some duration, which it turned out to be. I got the lieutenant on the phone and told him it didn't look good for today either. I waded through the silence that spelled his unhappiness. I never looked forward to talking with the lieutenant. The only pleasure it gave me was that I seemed to just naturally infuriate him.

"He's a sorry looking son-of-a-bitch, Houser," I said. "Puking, shitting, fainting away... not the sort of person you'd want in the back of your car. By the way, little Stacey and her woeful mother have set up camp at the chief's door. The kid won't leave without seeing her true love, and her mother looks pretty much powerless to influence her one way or the other."

"They are not our problem," said the lieutenant.

"Yes, sir, just bringing you up to date. By the way, I had to pepper spray her."

"Who?"

"Stacey. She grabbed my arm."

"I wish you wouldn't do that."

"I wish she wouldn't interfere, but she seems determined to do same."

"Can you concentrate on Houser? He's the felon."

"Oh, he has my complete attention. I'm not sure I can say the same for Odd."

"Odd? What's with Gunderson?"

"Nothing."

"You brought it up. Out with it. What?"

"You know Odd."

"Quinn, don't bust my balls."

"Oh, it's this old-timey murder case they got here. Odd's playing detective, thinks he can solve the case. It's older than he is and colder than you are."

"A murder case?"

"Affirm."

"And he thinks he can solve it? Gunderson?"

"He's gone all dreamy on it. I mean, he's fine and all, but there ain't much for us to do except wait for Houser to stop puking. So in the meantime, Odd's been playing detective."

"Tell him not to do that."

"Yes, sir."

"Tell him to stay out of people's way."

"Will do."

"How long's it gonna take?"

"What?"

"For Houser to stop puking."

"I'll ask the medicine man."

"Don't bust my balls, Quinn!"

"Sorry, Lieutenant."

Just then, Odd came up to me with a piece of golden frybread sitting on a napkin, oozing grease. "Have this while it's hot," he said. "It's Indian bread. Delish." He gave it to me and went back, not at all interested in what was transpiring over the wire.

Since the lieutenant had fallen back into his silent mode, I bit into the hot greasy bread, and it really was a wonderful thing to have in your mouth. I knew I was going to eat the rest of it, which I would then wear, not have on my thighs.

"Are you eating something, talking to me?" asked the lieutenant.

"Sorry, Lieutenant. It's Indian frybread. We're at the chief's house."

He took another moment and said, "Maybe you should extend the chief a professional courtesy."

"Begging your pardon, sir, but what would that be?"

"Maybe you should help them with their murder case."

"Excuse me? First of all, it isn't really their case. It's the Sheriff's case, even though one of the two kids killed was an Indian, and it might have been a hate crime, in the days before they had that classification. Now that I think about it, what crime isn't a hate crime? You got money and I don't—I hate you."

"Quinn, you're bustin' my balls."

"Second, and sorry about that, they don't want our help because nobody is working on the case. In their wisdom, they all have accepted that sometimes someone gets away with murder. And third, what would be the value of our professional courtesy since neither one of us knows jack-shit about investigating a murder, even if it happened last night instead of thirty-three years ago."

"But you said Gunderson could help them."

"I said he thought he could solve the case, but that's Odd. Odd might say he thought he could hold his breath for six minutes."

"Can he do that?"

"It was just an example."

"You say that Houser can't travel much before tomor-row morning?"

"That's affirm. He looks like shit on a clothesline."

"Okay, then. Get a room, nothing too expensive. Keep your receipts. Keep close watch on Houser's condition. Don't let them give him up unless it looks like he's cashin' his check. Officially, as of now, you're on loan to the chief there, so help him with this murder. A kind of cross-cultural hands-across-the-state sort of a deal."

"Lieutenant, there ain't no murder case, at least not that the chief has. You haven't been listening. Is it because I'm a woman?"

"No, Quinn, it's because you're black."

For the record, I am not black. Polish on my mother's side, Irish on my father's. About the time the Irish were getting out of the coal mines, the Polish were filling them up. My folks met in the change. The lieutenant was just cracking wise about discrimination in general.

"Where's Gunderson been getting his information on the murder thing?"

"From the chief, but..."

"Well, there you have it."

"Have what, for fuck's sake?"

"Quinn, the mouth."

"Sorry, but I am two minutes away from a conniption with the conniption fast gaining."

"Let us review. And I'm taking notes. On this day we had a conversation. Substance being, Houser is suffering an intestinal disorder, the result of a self-inflicted bite. Your call is not to make him travel thusly. As your superior, I concur. So as to justify your staying over, apart from monitoring Houser, you request and I authorize a temporary duty assignment, that being to assist the reservation police in examining evidence relative to a crime committed upon one of their members at some time past. How's that sound?"

Like overrefined bullshit that has lost its power to fertilize.

"That sounds just lovely, Lieutentant," which due to the tone of my voice conveyed the same message.

"Would you like me to check in?" I asked.

"Only if you can't help yourself," he answered.

8

This particular tribe had come to accept casino gambling and the resale of fireworks, but they drew the line at hotel management, believing it was wrong to make a person pay for sleeping in your bed. The only overnight accommodations were on the white part of the island, The Tidewater Cottages, four tiny cottages in need of paint and repair, owned and managed by Frank and Angie Rupert, who met us at the driveway. Chief Shining Pony had called ahead.

Frank moved with difficulty, half crippled with lower back pain. He used Angie's wheelchair for support as he pushed her over the gravel. She was obese and crippled by her own bulk. After the introductions, Frank told us we were lucky indeed because they had one cottage vacant, a rarity at this time of the year, the start of the tourist season. It was The Honeymoon Cottage and went for seventy-five dollars a night. I must have reacted.

"Too high?" said Frank.

Looking at the run-down place with its little splintered porch out front, I admitted it did sound a bit dear for the goods. "Never go cheap on your honeymoon is my advice," said the innkeeper. "It'll taint the marriage."

I opened my arms to call his attention to my uniform. "Does it look like we're on a honeymoon here, Frank?"

"Could be. We've had couples show up on Kawasakis and in scuba gear. We had a witch and a warlock. We had a gent on social security with his nineteen-year-old bride. We had the skinniest black man I ever seen with a white woman that made Angie here look pet-teet!"

"Trust me, Frank, we're not on our honeymoon."

"I don't know, Quinn," said Odd, "we say we're on our honeymoon, we might get special treatment."

Frank laughed at Odd's ingenuity and assured us that all their guests get the same special treatment. I told him we'd take the cottage.

"How many nights would that be for?"

"Just tonight."

"Just one night?" said Angie. "Why, that hardly gives you a chance to get the flavor of the island."

"We already got some of the flavor," I said.

"You stay awhile, you won't ever want to leave," she told us.

I wanted to leave hours ago. I never wanted to come here in the first place.

"Good place to settle down and live?" asked Odd.

"Only one requirement... you gotta like rain!" The infirm couple shared a laugh.

"Much crime on the island?" asked Odd.

They laughed again. "Crime? My Lord, everybody knows everybody and what criminal wants to make his getaway on that slow-as-molasses ferry!"

"We heard about that double-murder...," said Odd.

They looked at each other, wide-eyed. Murder? Double murder?

"James and Jeannie?"

"James and Jeannie? Oh, my stars," said Frank, leaning heavier on the wheelchair, "that was ages ago. You're talking ancient history. You had me going there for a minute, son. Murder, indeed. I do believe that was the last murder on this island."

"Of innocent people," added Angie.

"Any idea who might have pulled the trigger?"

"None at the time, none now. Can't believe it was an islander, though. Down there in America, sure, they got the serial killers down there, wanderin' around just looking for someone to snuff."

"You think that's what happened, some crazed mainlander came over, stumbled upon them... carrying a shotgun?"

"We'll never know, son. Not now, not after all these years."

The sky grew dark and I thought it would rain shortly so I asked them for the key.

"Oh, we don't have keys here. I'd be surprised if anybody on the island even remembers where their house key is. I can't let you in yet anyhow. The other folks haven't checked out." Frank lowered his voice. "They been in there five days. Hey, maybe you better look in and make sure nobody's murdered them in their sleep!" Frank and Angie laughed. "Though if you ask me, there hasn't been a whole lot of sleep going on in there, if you know what I mean!"

Angie suggested we take a tour of the island, have lunch at the cafe, which she could recommend, and come back around one o'clock. By that time our cottage would be ready. We made a move to get back into the car, but Frank said, "Not so fast."

Angie pulled out a clipboard from the side of her wheelchair and clicked open a ballpoint pen. "There's a few things we have to know first," she said. "Like, do you prefer white wine or red?"

Odd and I looked at each other. "We prefer beer," I said.

Angie did not break stride.

"Canadian or American?" she asked.

Da frick. Canadian, okay?

"Would you like flannel sheets or plain cotton?"

I looked at Odd and thankfully he jumped in and said, "Look, how many beds are in that cottage?"

"How many beds?" said Frank. "It's the honeymoon cottage! There's only the one."

"You take the bed, Quinn. You decide what sheets."

"Do you have a rollaway bed?" I asked them.

"You don't even wanna sleep in the same bed?" asked Frank.

"We're not lovers," I said. "Look at us, I'm old enough to be his mother."

"Not that old," said Odd.

"I have a twenty-two-year-old son in the Navy, for cripessake. Look, we're working partners. We had no plans to stay over; it just turned out that way."

"I still have to know what kind of sheets you want," said Angie.

Flannel sheets were so nice to the touch but they might make me hot. And what was I going to sleep in? I'd have to wash out my skivvies overnight, which put me in that bed in the buff, and Odd in the same room. What if I got hot and kicked away the flannel sheets? Why does everything get so complicated as we get older?

"Just plain cotton," I said, finally.

"Really? Most people prefer flannel."

"Yeah, well...."

"Plain sheets it is."

We tried to make our escape, but she had one more preference to nail down. "What about music? Country? Soft rock...?"

I shut the door, started up the car. "Forget about the music; we brought our own," I said through the open window, thinking about Odd's tapes.

Angie smiled knowingly. "Brought your own music, hey?" she said, looking up to her husband. "I believe someone is not being entirely honest with us."

"Or with themselves!" chortled Frank.

We did wind up taking a kind of random tour of the island, in a light rain, down a little winding country road lined with tall cedars. We passed the Tribal Headquarters, the most imposing edifice on the island, and a few intersections of small commerce: a grocery store and video rental joint combined, an auto repair shop, a small nursery, the sheriff's sub-station.

"Can you believe those two? I wonder what their story is," I said.

"I'm sure we'll find out," said Odd.

"Not if I can help it. They give me the creeps. How could they believe you and I... came in uniform... looking to shack up... you, your age, and... me?"

"You're a good-looking woman, Quinn, you'd have no trouble finding a guy in his thirties."

I flushed. My ears were about to blow off. He had no idea. "What would I do with one?"

"The usual stuff."

"I'm gonna slap you silly."

"You never thought about it?"

"I'm a married woman, da frick."

"Well, that's a tribute to Connors."

How does he know what I've thought about or what I haven't thought about? And I loved the way he attributed everything to Connors.

"A thirty-year-old man," I told him, "is about twice as mature as a fifteen-year-old boy, which puts him at about eighteen. Don't need one, don't want one."

"I was only paying you a compliment."

"Save it for someone who'll believe it."

We found ourselves on the back edge of a boatyard, and a haphazard arrangement of boats on stands, some tarped over. Suddenly Odd said, "Stop the car! Stop! Here!"

I pulled over. "What's wrong?"

"That boat..." he said. We were looking at a derelict of a fishing boat, blistered and broken, no longer seaworthy. He got out of the car and looked at it through the chain link fence. I killed the engine and joined him there. The boat was called *Northern Comfort.*

"Yeah, it's an old boat. What about it?"

"I know this boat. I've seen it before."

"Where?"

"I can't remember."

Then, after a moment, he said, "I know who owns this boat, who skippered it for a living."

"Who?"

"This was Frank's boat."

"Frank from Frank and Angie?"

"He made his living on this boat, crabbing."

"Frank, the weird innkeeper? The man's half-crippled."

"Yeah, he got that way working on this boat... the *Northern Comfort.* It was a good boat in its day."

"When did he say anything about a crabbing boat?"

I knew the answer. He never did. Odd was not hearing me. He went off in his dreamy way and said, "The money was good. Crabbing was profitable. James Coyote crewed for him one summer. That's how he was able to buy the pick-up. But Frank was a hard skipper and the work was too dangerous."

My nipples went hard. They damn near pulled me through the windshield. Lately, my body was not my own, but this was ridiculous.

"Odd, you're giving me the willies. How the hell do you know that?"

We sat there looking at each other with blank eyes, two scared cops, and neither one of us scared easily.

"Ever since we came on this island," he said, "I've been feeling... unsettled, and then seeing that picture of those two kids, something clicked. Now, looking at that boat.... Don't ask me how, but I know this stuff."

"How can you?"

"I just do."

"Anything like this ever happen before?"

"Never."

"Psychics don't run in your family or anything...?"

"My family? In my family, you have a vision, you get an enema."

I couldn't help laughing. "You had a vision?"

"No, just a strong sense... a knowledge, of something I know, about this place and these people, but I don't know why I know it, or even what I know. This is freaking me out, Quinn."

"Let's just go sit in the car for a minute, okay? Let's take a quiet look at all this. No visions, no voices."

"I'm going crazy, ain't I?"

"Look, you haven't slept all night and you don't sleep well anyway. You've got major sleep disorders. You take the bed. Let's go back, get you to bed, sleep all day. We got nothing to do but wait for Houser to stop puking."

"But I'm not sleepy, not at all. I feel... urged... pushed on by something. There's something we gotta do here, Quinn; there's a reason why we came to this island. And we don't have much time."

Time? I looked at my watch. Connors was expecting me home by now. I tried to call him on my cell, but of course there was no reception out there in the deep water hard against Canada.

We found a Jiffy Mart with a public phone. I used my AT&T card to make the call. Through the front window, I could see Odd chatting up the Indian woman behind the counter.

"Pharmacy," answered Esther, all pert and a pain in the ass.

"I need to talk to Connors, Esther."

"Hi, Girlfriend, wuzzup?"

I got your girlfriend, bitch. Put my husband on the phone or I'll break your jaw. That's the inner dialog. What I said was, "I can't talk to you now, Esther; this is kind of an emergency."

"Oh…"

She quickly buzzed or nodded or gave Connors a look, because in a second he came on with a worried tone. I explained I was still on Geronimo Acres waiting out a sick prisoner and would have to spend the night. I didn't get into what was happening with Odd, figuring it would be something we could talk about tomorrow night over a couple of Rolling Rocks.

"You sound out of breath," he said.

"I do? No, I'm fine."

"Do you have a number?" he asked.

"A number?"

"Where you'll be staying."

"Oh, where we'll be staying... I doubt there's even a phone in that place."

I didn't tell him it was the Honeymoon Cottage or about the goofy couple there were encouraging me to hop into bed with Odd.

"Listen, Connors, they only have the one cabin, so we got to share. Odd volunteered for the davvy, gave me the bed, but I might have to insist, 'cause he hasn't slept in I don't know how long... but either way, don't worry, 'cause, you know, there won't be any funny business going on."

I was coming unglued, but he laughed and said, "I know that."

"Well, you don't have to be so happy about it."

"You think I'm happy? I'd be happy if you did find someone who could light your fire. Lord knows, I can't."

"It's not you, Connors; how many times do I have to explain that? It has nothing to do with you. It's me. I've lost it. No man in the world can bring it back. I'm sorry."

"This is probably not a good time for this conversation."

"Probably not," I agreed.

"You should have the bed. Odd is young; he'll be fine on the sofa. You get that numbness in your legs, you don't sleep right."

I wanted him to express some... what, jealousy? He didn't care at all that for the first time in our marriage I would be sharing a room with another man. Why should he? I'd be safe with Harrison Ford, da frick. But he was wishing something would happen, wishing that an attractive younger man might awaken what died in me. I was there for him; I'd be a good sport once a month, but that part of me was gone. Not he or anyone else was ever going to bring it back. It was just how life would be from now on.

"Well, whatever," I said. "I know you're busy, so…."

"You know what you should do? You should get out of that uniform, buy yourself something comfortable to wear."

It's not what I wanted to hear. More and more, with each year, he was saying things I didn't want to hear, and not saying the things I did want to hear.

"I will," I said. "It is getting a little gamey by now, and while we're waiting, we're not on duty, not officially."

"What are you going to do with yourself, stuck out there?"

"Beats me."

"Get some rest. Take a one-day vacation."

"Sure. I have to go now."

"Okay," he said. "Be careful."

He was sleeping with Esther. I was sure of it. He would sleep with her tonight.

I hung up with that little-bit-lost feeling, orphaned inside. I tried to shake it off. I hated that feeling. I'd rather be shot, which I was once, and it felt not near as bad.

Odd came out of the Jiffy Mart and we both walked to the car.

"How's Connors?" he asked.

"Fine. Anything happen in the Jiffy Mart?"

"Like what?"

"Like you saw stuff that you knew."

"Go into any Jiffy Mart, you're gonna see stuff that you know."

"Don't get wise with me."

"The place has only been here twelve years."

"What difference would that make?"

"I seem to be going back further than that."

"Like to the time of the murders?"

"I think so."

We drove back to the white part of the island and found a horsey shop that also sold clothes. All I wanted was a pair of jeans, a T-shirt, and something heavier against the chill that would come with evening. They had a draped off corner for a changing room, and we took turns in it. The jeans were all Wranglers, which I hadn't seen since I was a kid back in Pennsylvania. My service shoes were black Rockports which went fine with the jeans. I got a T-shirt with a tribal bear on it and a hooded sweatshirt. I put it all on the Visa. I knew the Lieutenant would trash it as an expense item, but he was going to get it anyway. He could have the clothes too, if he wanted them. Odd also got jeans and a Shalish Island T-shirt and a light Eddie Bauer windbreaker that folded up into its own pocket. It was a great relief to get out of the uniforms, which we put on hangers and lay neatly in the trunk of the Lumina. We stashed our belts and pistols, flashlights and batons. I felt a ton lighter.

The cafe was across the street. I was thinking I might treat myself to pie. Odd was two steps behind me. I looked over my shoulder and saw him taking it in, the cafe, in his dreamy way of having seen it all before. It wasn't much to look at. Exposed to the salt air, it needed paint, like most of the structures we'd seen. There were a couple old-timey soda signs in the windows, like "Moxie."

Going into that cafe, we looked like mother and son in spanking new jeans, mom with a hooded sweatshirt. Which I quickly pulled off because the place was overheated. The T-shirt tried to come off with it, exposing my belly, and suddenly a dozen limp-dicks at the counter were interested. Da frick. Half of them were old Indians, the other half maybe fishermen who didn't go out that day.

Free of the sweatshirt, I saw Odd sitting down at a booth at the window. I followed him. We sat on opposite sides of the table. He gripped the edge of it and leaned toward me and whispered, "You're not going to believe this, Quinn."

"I'm ready to believe anything."

"I've been here before."

"No, you haven't."

"Yes, I have."

"On the island?"

"In this cafe, in this booth."

My nipples popped again. Sweat trickled down my cleavage. I took a fingerful of T-shirt and pulled it away, fanning some air down over my chest.

The waitress was a woman in her thirties, but they were hard years. She asked us first if we wanted coffee.

"Iced tea," I said. I was burning up.

"And for you?"

Odd shook his head, lost his voice.

I watched him until she came back with the iced tea, but he never said anything. Soon, a pleasantness came over his features. They softened, relaxed.

"So…, what will you have?" asked the waitress.

"You bake your own pie?" I asked.

"Yes, ma'am," she said proudly.

"Apple?"

"Fresh today."

"That's for me, a la mode."

"I'll have a black 'n tan," said Odd.

Both the waitress and I looked at him and huh?

"A what?" she asked.

"A black 'n tan."

"What's that?" she asked.

"He'll know," said Odd.

"Joey," she called to the kitchen. "Do you have a black 'n tan?"

Joey, a recovering alcoholic in his late twenties, poked his head through the pass-through window. His head was covered with a Harley Davidson wrap. He yelled back, "Say what?"

"A black 'n tan."

"Never heard of it."

An old Indian man at the counter said, "They used to make them here. Long ago. The Stauffers owned this place then."

"Right," said Odd, "like when the Stauffers had it."

"A black 'n tan," said the old Indian, "is an ice cream sundae. Vanilla ice cream with chocolate sauce on the bottom. Then carmel. Crushed up peanuts. A blossom of whipped cream. A cherry on the top."

"That's it! Thank you, sir," said Odd.

My nipples had not gone down. On the contrary, the rest of me was straining to pop out as well, like my whole body was on a countdown to explode. I wanted to go screaming through the rain.

"I'd like to try that," said the waitress, and for a second I thought she had read my mind. No, Odd had inspired her. She was like a cynical bartender who had discovered a new drink.

After she left, I said, "Odd," and there was a quaver to my voice, "what the hell is going on here?"

"You know how something happens and you say, whoa, all this has all happened before?"

"Yeah, it's called *déjà-vu*, which is about all the French I know."

"This isn't like that. I know this place. I know these people."

"No, you don't."

"I do. I used to sit in this booth. How can that be, unless…?"

"Unless what?"

"Unless I was one of them once."

"So, who's the old guy, then?"

I nodded to the old Indian who had remembered the ice cream sundae. Odd looked at him hard. I was about to tell him he didn't know shit, when he called out, "Mr. Drinkwater!"

The old man turned on his counter stool. "Yes, sir?"

"Thank you very much!"

"You're welcome."

I held my head in my hands, much like Stacey's mother had when I first saw her, like events had overtaken her, and now me, and things were spinning out of control, and maybe if I squeezed my head very hard everything would get forced back to normal. I felt columns of sweat worming over my ribs.

"I had a life before this one," Odd said, "and I spent it here on this island."

"That ain't the way it works," I said, "not where we come from." Meaning basically, I guess, from good Catholic and Lutheran families.

"When I was a kid, I was told a lot of stuff about life and death that turned out to be lies."

"Yeah, well, me too," I admitted, "but you're talking…," I could hardly bring myself to say it, "…reincarnation. Are you really ready to believe that stuff?"

"I never thought about it before, but one life does sound like kind of a short deal, doesn't it? Just about the time you get your poop in a group, it's over. Why shouldn't we get another crack at it, keep trying 'til we get it right? That would make some sense."

"That doesn't make any sense. What would be the point of living?"

"No, otherwise, what would be the point of dying?"

Woi Yesus. Was this ever a conversation I didn't want to have.

"I knew this place before we ever landed on it. I knew about Frank's boat, Jimmy crewing…"

"We don't know if that's true."

"Oh, we know, we know."

I knew I wouldn't bet against it.

The waitress came back with my pie and his ice cream sundae.

"Whaddaya think?" she said.

"That's it," said he. "That's exactly it."

I was slow to dig into my pie. An uncharacteristic sudden loss of appetite. I watched as Odd began his approach to the sundae, the black 'n tan. He ate a couple spoonfuls and looked up at me.

"Well?" I asked.

"Too sweet and gooey. I never did like desserts and sweets much. I like salted stuff."

"This time around," I said, a little sarcastically.

"Don't bust my balls, Quinn."

Enough guys say that to me enough times, and one day I'm likely to believe I am a ball-buster, but that day hasn't come yet.

"Let's say you were one of these yonkos, in your other life. Which one were you? I mean, what if you were the old hermit, who lived on the hill? What if you killed those kids, I mean, in that life? You gonna turn yourself it? They gonna prosecute you?"

"Don't be ridiculous…, but if I am, then don't I have

to find a way to remove the stain… somehow?"

I gave him a withering look, and he snapped at me.

"Look, dammit, if it's not that, what is it?"

"Intuition, good guesses, a little psychic stuff working, everybody's supposed to have some. ESP and all that."

"This is way beyond ESP. Way. It's like we were sent here by somebody or something for a specific reason."

"We were! Da frick! We were sent by the lieutenant to bring home Charles T. Houser. And, by God, that's what we're gonna do tomorrow morning, if I have to sit next to him and hold the bucket while he pukes."

"We still have 'til then," said Odd.

9

In the ladies' room, I pulled off my bear T-shirt and wiped myself down with moist paper towels, trying to lower my whacked-out thermostat. I said a few Hail Mary's and Our Father's by rote but not without sincerity. The soul is not something I never thought about before, even doubted after a particularly bad day on the job, but I always wound up accepting the trajectory as laid out by the church: it comes into being at conception, occupies a vessel for the blink of an angel's eye, and then ascends into heaven or descends into hell or gets lodged for a million years in purgatory. The recycling of the soul was the stuff of tabloid papers and cheesy TV shows, not something to be taken seriously. And yet, at a certain level, it sounded good. Who ever gets it right in just one lifetime? And what better way to walk in someone else's shoes than to walk in someone else's body? But do the math. There are five billion people in the world, soon there will be six billion. Where do the extra billion souls come from? Unless it's not one soul each. Maybe we all share the same soul matter, and share it with all living things.

By the time I came out of the ladies', the lunch crowd was filling the cafe. More idle fishermen, more old Indians, some retirees in for the specials. Odd had given up our table and was standing at the end of the counter talking to the old man who had remembered the Stauffers and the sundae thing.

I was on my way to collar him when I saw Frank wheel in Angie and head for the last vacant table, where Angie's chair would replace one of the cafe's. They didn't recognize me until I was next to them.

"Well, look at you," squealed Angie. "Don't you look cute? Now, you're fitting right in, aren't you?"

"Where's your…'partner'?" asked Frank. I was beginning to think a leer was his permanent facial pattern.

"At the counter, makin' friends."

They swiveled around and found Odd.

"Oh, doesn't he look good, too? Isn't he a hunk?" said Angie.

"Old man Drinkwater," said Frank. "He'll talk your ear off. Have you had lunch? They have a killer tuna melt here. Join us."

"We already had something," I said. "What's the word on our cottage?"

"Well, the word on your cottage is… it's yours," said Frank happily. "Go for it."

"There's Molsons in the fridge and cotton sheets on the bed and the Bee Gees on the hi-fi, just so you don't have to go into a strange and quiet place," Angie added.

"Great. Listen, Frank, I'm curious. What kind of work were you in before you started running the cottages?"

"Why, do I seem out of my element as an innkeeper?"

"A little, I guess. I just had the feeling you once did something… outdoorsy."

"As outdoorsy as you can get, little lady. I fished crab for years in the Bering Sea, and lived to tell about it."

"He was a wild one, he was," said Angie.

My spine struck high C. Down the front ran the sweat-works again.

"I laid away a nice nest egg, sold the boat, bought the cottages. Now you have the complete story of my life."

"Oh, you held back a few things," said a devilish Angie.

"You hush now."

"You had a boat?"

"Oh, you can't crab without a boat. Your arms get tired."

He and the missus cracked up. I could see the secret to their marriage.

"Did your boat have a funny name?"

"Only yachts have funny names. Fishin' is deadly serious, and the boats are christened accordingly."

I was glad to learn that.

Then he went on: "'*Northern Comfort*' could be ironic, I guess, but it wasn't meant to be."

Woi Yesus. I'd already heard enough to know my life would never again be quite the same, the way it has to change once you've seen a ghost or a flying saucer or some other thing you know cannot exist. You wind up spending the rest of your life retelling the story, hoping someone will believe you, which is kind of what I'm doing right now, this keyboard on my lap, the snow falling outside my window.

I went the extra fathom with Frank.

"Did that boy, James Coyote, ever crew for you?"

"Isn't that something?" trilled Angie. She looked at the old skipper and clapped her hands once. "After you left, we started talking about that old murder... that awful tragedy."

"Yeah, and I remembered," said Frank, "how James crewed for me one summer. He made big money for those days and bought himself a used Ford four-by, still in high school. He told me he wouldn't be going out with me the next season. All he wanted to do was ride his four-by and chase after white girls."

"Oh, he didn't say that either," said Angie.

"No, he said he couldn't go out again 'cause he was flat-out scared to. There's no shame in that. Every man who goes crabbing up there is scared, but they weigh the risk against the reward and they go out anyway. I really ex-pected James would too, but by the time the season rolled around again, somebody had blown off his head."

Woi Yesus again. I was an abbreviated boo away from flinging off my clothes and running naked through the rain.

I collected Odd at the end of the counter and told him we had to get outside or else I was going to disappear in a flash of flame. On the sidewalk I saw that he had the old Indian man in tow, his hand under his arm, half guiding, half supporting.

"He says he knows me... from before."

Woi Yesus a third time.

"Where are we taking him?"

"He's taking us."

The old man had to sit in the back, in the cage, but it seemed to make no great difference to him. He was secure in his cosmic innocence. To worry about him talking off your ear had to be another of Frank's lame jokes, because he didn't say anything except to direct us, finally to one more dirt road that dipped into a wetlands, though the whole island seemed wetlands to me. When we got to where we were going, the drizzle stopped and the sun broke through. I put on my shades.

A large black mongrel with wet matted hair barked menacingly at our arrival, out of a sense of duty, apparently, because he seemed happy to see us once we alit from the car, his tail wagging, his head down for a pat. A cat on the porch licked her paw. A rooster and his harem of hens scratched about within leaping distance of the cat but were unafraid.

Old man Drinkwater asked us to wait while he went inside.

It was a poor house, one tiny room added to another over the years, one shed of plywood and sheet metal constructed after another, as the need arose and the materials afforded. I had been measuring my breath ever since getting out of the car. Now standing there, looking at the house, waiting for its occupants, I was pretty much holding it in. In spite of the face I'd been putting on, I had all but bought into Odd's experience. Maybe later I would be able to sort out some other explanation, but for the moment I was swept up into it and it was hard not to believe that Odd had led another life, and it had been on this ground.

Earlier I warned him that he could have been the number one suspect. It never occurred to me, until that moment, at the Coyote house, that he might have been the victim. I watched him for any signs of recognition. I didn't see any. The dog had certainly taken to him, rubbing up against his leg as Odd roughed up his ear, and he was an old dog, but he was not that old.

"Odd? What are we supposed to say to these people?"

"I was hoping you'd know. You're senior."

Before I could smack him upside the head, Drinkwater came out with a couple almost as old as he. They were rail thin, the woman from wear, the man from disease. A hose connected his nostrils to a tank of oxygen he moved with a hand truck. This was an island of infirms, I thought. They looked at us from the porch and we looked at them from the yard until our host waved us feebly to join them on the porch, where there was enough seating to accommodate a small pow-wow: a rusty metal glider, several plastic molded chairs, chaise lounges made from rubber tubing, a few overturned milk crates, and a bench seat from an old pickup, the terrycloth seat covers still on it. This was the most comfortable spot and was offered to Odd and me. You had to lower yourself to one knee to get on it, then stretch your legs out in front.

I don't know what old Drinkwater had told them; I don't know what he knew or what went on between him and Odd while I was hosing myself down in the ladies' room. We sat on the porch and said nothing for some moments, watching the vapor rise from the back of the black dog as the newly emerged sun hit it.

The old dog broke the ice by bringing a soggy tennis ball and dropping it at Odd's feet. He threw it over the porch railing and the dog leaped after it.

"Now you're in for it," said Mr. Coyote.

"They're from Spokane," said our guide.

"We used to go there, to dance," said Mr. Coyote.

I had decided, for once, I was going to keep my mouth shut.

"We're policemen there," said Odd, then corrected himself, "...police persons." I wanted to smack him again. "We got here last night, on police business. And it looks like we'll be going back tomorrow." All three of the Indians nodded their heads solemnly. Odd threw the ball again for the dog. "Last night, at the tribal police headquarters, I got interested in your case, James' case... his murder." They nodded again, in the same way, as though both comments drafted the same water. "Do you mind talking about it?"

James' parents took a moment and without looking at each other said, "No," simultaneously, and our old guide said something in their own language, which in the world is probably spoken by about a hundred and twenty-two people. Whatever he said, it made a hell of an impression on them. I couldn't take it. I had to ask.

"I told them this young man used to live here," said Drinkwater, "before he was the person he is now. I knew him back then."

"Why didn't you say it in English?" My stomach was hurting, like maybe I'd had a bad clam, even though I'd had nothing to eat since frybread, if you don't count those two nervous bites of pie a la mode.

"It makes more sense in Shalish," he said.

I got it. I knew a little Polish, not enough to explain this, but I knew it would make even less sense in Polish. My mother's people kept their eyes on the potato, their brogues on the ground. It was the Irish half of me playing havoc with my grasp on reality.

Odd asked the old couple to tell us about their son, dead these more than thirty years now. The father, whose name was David, said his son's name was James Coyote. He died when he was seventeen, a senior in the local high school. He was the second oldest of four brothers. Two of his brothers are still on the island, but Warren, the youngest, went to Las Vegas and became a dealer of blackjack. Having said all that, he stopped talking. Either that was all he had to say or all he could say until refueled with more oxygen.

"Did he have any enemies?" asked Odd. I don't know what book he was playing from, but it seemed like a reasonable question.

The parents looked to our guide, as though he may be better able to field that question. "We are all family here," he volunteered. "We have our disagreements, but we eat the same food, sleep under the same sky. To kill my son would be to kill your own, to kill yourself. James was killed by a white man."

Why was I part of this? I felt embarrassed and ashamed to watch this frail old couple put through this. They had lost a son. I still had a son.

"Then, did he have any enemies among the whites?" asked Odd.

"Yes," said his father, "One."

We looked at him dumbly, but it had no effect on him. "And who would that be?" I asked, finally.

"Someone who did not want him with that girl."

If they seemed to know little about their deceased son, they knew nothing at all about his girlfriend, Jeannie Olson. It was a new romance, his first serious girlfriend, revealed to them by one of the brothers, who teased James about it because she was white and an inch taller than he. They had misgivings about it, not that such a thing had never happened before to other young people, and even some people not so young, but when it had it created awkward self-consciousness for the couple and contempt from the community and usually ended in shame and regret.

Our old guide said, "To quote Woody Allen, 'The heart goes where it wants to go.'"

I burst out laughing, I couldn't help it. The old guy smiled. Score one.

Odd fell into a lazy pattern of throwing the ball for the dog, a question here, a question there. I eased back into the cast-off seat of the totaled pickup, relieved that he had not yet opened his arms and cried, "Mom! Dad!" The old guide who claimed to have known him back then had

not yet put his finger on who he had been. It was like trying to remember a name that escapes you.

"What about that old hermit?" Odd asked.

"Wayne Coffey?"

"Was that his name?"

"Wayne was not a hermit," said Mr. Coyote. "He was
in my father's house, and my father was in his. It was only
later when he was old and tired of all the noise that people
started to talk about him. Wayne had no hatred in his heart
for anyone."

"Could be whoever did it is dead," I said.

The three Indians looked at me as though sorry for my
stupidity.

"No," said Odd, with authority, "he is not dead."

Now, they looked at him, but in a different way, like
he was the smart one.

"He?" said I. "How do you know it's a he?"

"Could a woman shotgun two innocent people?"

"Catch me on a bad day."

"It was a man," said Odd. Then, "I wish I could see
that pick-up they were in that night."

"It's out in the shed," the father said.

"You still have it?" asked Odd. I couldn't believe it
myself.

"You can't sell a vehicle somebody's died in unless you
sell it to a white man, and I couldn't do that."

We stepped through the mud to one of the several sheds,
this one big enough to hold a car. The dog had given up on
the game, but followed Odd's heels as if trying to impress

a new master. It was slow going because James' father had to wheel his oxygen tank through the mud, but once outside the shed it was all gravel. I stomped the mud off my Rockports. The woman swung open the two wooden doors to the shed.

"It's under that," said David, that being a dusty blue tarp. Odd took one corner, I took the other, and we pulled the tarp away, laying it out on the gravel. The truck was white, scarred and dinged, with a canopy over the bed, and spread on the bed was a mover's blanket. There was little room left in the shed for anything else, though spare parts hung from nails in the walls.

"Can we push it out into the light?" asked Odd.

"You can," said David. "I'll watch."

The vehicle was already in neutral. Odd and I got behind it and leaned backwards. I put a muddy foot against the far wall. Odd did likewise, and we flexed that four-by off the spot it had stuck to for over thirty years. It broke free and rolled easily out of the shed, coming to rest over the tarp on the gravel.

I believe the natural inclination of anyone looking at a vehicle for the first time would be to look into the driver's side window. That's what I did. You look at where you would sit if you had this car. You look at the steering wheel, where your hands would be. You might check the mileage from there. That was my theory, still is, but Odd got into the passenger seat without any hesitation.

No way would I get into that vehicle, either side. Dry and hardened blood, and if I'm not mistaken, brain matter, was all over the dash, the seats, the passenger window, and the back window. He ignored all that and settled himself into the seat. He shut the door and turned his head a few times, as though trying to click into a position, which he did finally: looking across the imaginary driver and through the open window, at me.

He put his hand to his throat and swallowed hard. "Something's wrong here," he said.

"What?" said I.

"That window is open."

"Yes," said the father.

"And this one closed?" The passenger window was all but opaque with dried blood and specks of other stuff.

"Everything is like it was."

"The killer must have gone to the driver's side," I said. "Shot James, then Jeannie."

"No, something's wrong. They talked to the killer through the open window. They knew him."

"Maybe the window was open 'cause they wanted some air. They were necking; the place got steamed up," I said.

"No, they would have just cracked it then. It was raining that night, hard. They wouldn't roll the window all the way down unless they were talking to someone, unless they knew who they were talking to. The killer stood on that side. They talked to him. Then Jeannie clutched Jimmy's arm, so hard she left bruises there."

Jimmy?

Odd's hands seemed to clutch at an imaginary arm, and they trembled. They were out of his control, shaking in the air, clutching to nothing. His eyes glazed over. There was a terror on his face I had never seen before. In fact, it was no longer his face. That expression of fear did not, could not, come from Odd Gunderson. I was standing where the killer would have been, so he was looking at me, and never in my life have I engendered such fear in another human being, but, of course, it wasn't me. It was whoever Odd was seeing where I was standing.

"Who are you looking at? " I asked him. "What's his name? Odd? Odd? Who is it?"

When I said his name, his head jerked sideways in an involuntary spasm, and he was back. The face was Odd's again.

"Something's wrong," he said.

Across the hood of the car, I looked at the old Indian who had brought us here, Drinkwater, and I thought I saw in him the flash of recognition.

10

I made the decision I was in the better condition to drive, and so I did, back to the part of the island under county jurisdiction. Our old Indian guide wanted to take us himself to Karl's Auto Repair, but I settled for directions instead. I told him, politely, to get on with the rest of his day.

The garage was easy to find. Seven cars were parked outside and two were up on lifts, a mechanic under each of them.

"Which one is Karl?" I asked Odd, as we approached, half testing, half already believing that of course he'd know.

"How should I know?" he said.

"Karl Gutshall?" I asked, when we got to the open bays.

The tall one on the right turned and came out from under the lift, looking us over. He wore greasy coveralls baggy in the butt and a gimme cap backwards on his head. He was my age. I noticed both the little and ring fingers of his left hand were missing. I wondered if anyone around here was still in one piece, and if we would be by the time we got off this damned island.

"What can I do for you?" he asked.

"We're from out of town."

"From the looks of your vehicle I would guess you're also cops."

"Oh, yeah, that too."

"Where're you from?"

"Spokane," I said.

He took off the cap and crumpled it into his back pocket. His hair was long, unkempt, and black. He was tall and stooped a bit and sad.

"But we're not here as cops," I said.

"Or maybe we are," said Odd.

"Odd, you got something you want to ask this man, as a police officer?"

"No, Quinn, you go ahead."

"Or otherwise?"

"Not just yet."

Odd might have needed to stand back and look at him for a while. After all, it was possible that this grease monkey had been his boyfriend in another life, thirty-some years ago. Something like that happened to me once, in the real world, when I went back to Pennsylvania to bury my mother and met up again with my high school boyfriend, "Our Johnny." Let me tell you, it was a major jolt. How'd he get so heavy? Where did all that rich wavy hair go? What were those gin blossoms doing on his nose? In Karl's case, I'd be wondering, how'd he lose those two fingers?

"We've just come from the Coyotes; you know them?" I asked him.

"Know them all. Which ones?"

"The old ones, David and his wife."

"Sure, I know them. Jimmy's folks."

"Jimmy's folks, right. We talked about this and that, sitting on their porch, threw a ball for the dog, and then we looked at Jimmy's old four-by.... They still have it, you know."

"Yeah, tribals can't sell a car somebody's died in."

"Anyway, we bounced around a couple ideas about how Jimmy and Jeannie wound up murdered...."

"You're here for that?"

"No, we're here on an entirely different matter, but since we had time to kill, we're visiting and talking and trying to come up with a profile of the kind of man who could shotgun two kids. The Coyotes didn't say much but they listened and after a while they came to understand that we were actually trying to figure out who did this thing. That's when they said to us, 'Everybody knows who did it.' Well, I was shocked. Weren't you shocked, Odd? A little? I mean, we spent all that time there and conjectured right and left and at the end of it, they say, everybody knows who killed their son. Karl Gutshall did it."

"They always did believe that," said Karl.

I was disappointed. I'd hoped to unhinge him a little.

"Why would they believe that?"

"It made sense to them, then, and they never let go of it. Not even when I was cleared by the police, who did their best to scare something out of me, and I was a scared kid, believe me, but you can't scare something out of a kid if it's not in him to begin with. I could never do anything like that, not then, not now, not ever."

"That's what they all say."

"I don't get it. Why are you here, two cops from Spokane?"

"You were Jeannie's boyfriend. She dumped you for James. You had a shotgun, recently fired. You had no alibi."

"So they did say, the Coyotes."

"They said that much."

"Okay, I don't know who you are, and it bothers me that after all these years I could be pulled away from my work to go through another third degree, and, Mister, you, I don't like the way you're boring a hole through me," he said, turning to Odd, "but let me bring you up to speed and then you can get the hell away from me."

"Take it easy; don't get all worked up."

"I didn't have an alibi because nobody who sleeps alone in his own bed had an alibi that night. It was the middle of the night. Everybody was home, asleep. That's my alibi. My mother, my father, my brother, we were all asleep. Sure, I had a shotgun, still do, most people on the island had a shotgun and most of them had been recently fired, because we had a rabbit problem you can't imagine. The more of 'em you shot, the more there were the next day. I don't ever want to eat rabbit again as long as I live. And, yes, Jeannie dumped me, but it wasn't for James."

Angry, he pulled his cap back out of his pocket, slammed it on his head, and rubbed it in. But he didn't go back to the Suburban he had up on the lift. I couldn't tell if he were steamed because of our intrusion or all over again because of what had happened to him back in high school. I couldn't tell if Odd was filled with lover's regret or simple pity.

"I'm sorry," Odd said.

"It was a long time ago."

"Not that long, though."

"Sometimes. Sometimes, not long enough by half. I loved that girl."

I waited for Odd to return the sentiment, but he held silent.

Karl went on, "If I knew who did that to Jeannie, I'd kill him with my bare hands."

Minus two fingers. I asked him, "If she didn't dump you for James, who then?"

"You guys want a Coke?"

We said we did. With the sun out it was getting a little warm for late May, sixty-one, -two, degrees.

He took off his cap again and stuffed it back into his pocket. It seemed to be his emotional abacus. He opened up the Coke machine with a key and pulled out three cold ones. We took them to a log bench down by the main road, put there I supposed for customers to sit and watch the traffic go by as they waited for their own rides to be serviced. Odd and I took the bench, Karl sat on a large painted white rock, his back to the southeastern flow of traffic, of which there was precious little, and not a bit more in the opposite direction, but what little there was slowed down to have a better look at us.

"Jeannie was, how do I put this...?" he said. "She matured earlier than a lot of us, earlier than me, for sure. We were crazy in love from the end of our junior year through the summer. She was ready, you know."

"Ready for what?" I asked.

"She was sexually ready. One night, in my father's car, she just went and put her hand on my…. I almost went through the roof. It was the sixties and everybody was doing it or talking about doing it or talking about how many times they'd already done it, but I was scared, frankly. I worried that I'd be too small, that I'd be too fast, too awkward all down the line, if you know what I mean."

I was surprised to hear a man my age recollect his youth in this way. At the same time I was dying to crack wise to Odd about what a slut he was in his former life, but I kept it zipped.

Odd said, "Do you still get the hiccups when you're nervous?"

Karl got them right then and there, had to put down his Coke, almost brought some of it up.

I patted him on the back and said, "It's a trick he does, don't let it rattle you."

It wouldn't rattle you if someone knew about every idiosyncracy? I urged him to go on, and finally he was able to, keeping one eye on Odd.

"What scared me most was the risk of losing her. I thought that if we did it, and it was bad, I would lose her; but if we didn't do it, and we had more time for her to, you know, get attached to my other qualities, we would have a better future together."

I was beginning to like this grease monkey. "So what did you do?"

"I moved her hand away and said pretty much what

I just said to you, and that if we loved each other we'd get to that when the time was right."

He was hiccuping all the way, until I said, "You were a sensible young man." After that, he wasn't nervous anymore, just regretful.

"I was an idiot. If I had done what she wanted, she might not have left me for someone who would, and it was that person who killed her. She might be alive today, if.... And me? Who knows? The only lesson I learned was, never refuse a willing woman."

"That's a fairly stupid lesson," I said.

"I won't argue it. But that's how I've lived my life. Married three of those willing women. Only because they asked me. Cheated on every one of them."

"You are an idiot."

"Yeah, but I'm not a murderer. Life could have been different, if only...."

"So who was this guy, then?"

"I wish I knew, because he's the one who murdered her. He murdered her because she dumped him for James."

"That one," said Odd, "was the man who taught her about making love, but that was all she wanted from him. She couldn't know all that he would want from her."

Karl Gutshall looked gut-shot. "What makes you know so much?" he said.

"It's a long story," said I. "Look, I'm assuming yours was a pretty small high school, ain't?"

"There were only twenty-eight kids in our graduating class."

"Do the math, do the elimination process. Who busted Jeannie's cherry?"

"Jesus, who are you?" said Karl, offended.

"You'd have to know who it was, small place like this."

"You did your best to find out back then," said Odd, boring another hole into Karl.

"Huh?" was all he could say.

"You were hurt and embarrassed and belittled and finally pretty pissed off, weren't you?"

Karl started hiccuping again. "I was a kid in high school. Ever happen to you?"

"You should have quietly sat and waited for all of that to pass away, but you let your anger consume you."

I didn't want Odd to go off on his sitting-still riff again. "What did he do with all that anger, Odd?" I asked.

"Huh?" said Karl.

"He followed her."

As I said, it was sixty-one, -two degrees, but sweat beaded out right there on Karl's forehead. Me, the usual spots: my butt, my armpits, my cleavage.

"You followed her!" Odd said, a girlish indignation in his voice, I swear. "You spied on her. You asked all her friends. You tried to break into her locker and read her secret notebook."

The way Odd held his breath in his sleep? That's what Karl was doing now, interrupted only by his hiccups.

"You were outraged," Odd laid into him. "Now you know it was yourself you were mad at, but back then you had to blame it all on her. You were so mad at her you could have killed her!"

The air exploded from Kart Gutshall. "But I didn't! I didn't!" He threw his half-full Coke bottle into the trees next to us. I never heard it break. "I didn't kill her. I loved her. I love her to this day."

"And you never found out who it was she gave herself to after you refused her."

"No, I never did, and neither did anyone else, not anyone else who was willing to come forward. Go back to Spokane. Leave me alone."

He walked in his sad gait back to his garage, in baggy coveralls, reaching back for his cap again and forcefully fitting it to his head.

"Thanks for the Cokes," I yelled after him.

He stepped under the shadow of the big Suburban and buried his head in its undercarriage.

Odd and I got back into the car, I behind the wheel. We sat for a moment. I didn't know where we would go next, but I knew where we must finally go eventually.

"You did know a bit about him," I said.

"Not enough."

"Here's what I don't get. Why can't you just say it? Just say who did it. You know so much; why don't you know that?"

"I have looked down the barrel of that shotgun. I have seen James' head blown away, all over me…. But I can't see who's holding the shotgun. If you asked me what kind of dancer he was, Karl, I could tell you. Lousy."

I had to chuckle. We were watching Karl as we spoke. You could tell he was rattled, trying to get his head back into his mechanics.

"You were no angel, though, were you?" I said, suppressing another chuckle. "Little Miss Hot Pants, grabbin' the boy's johnson."

He looked at me, rolled his eyes.

"What are we doing here, Quinn? Why'd the lieutenant pick us?"

"Shit detail, where's Quinn and Gunderson?"

"For that matter, why even Spokane? I've lived there my whole life and hated it. Why didn't I ever move somewhere else?"

"Hey, I married into it. Compared to Shenandoah, though, it's the Ritz. I always knew I would leave that place. I had to go, just felt pulled away, to the west. Never thought I'd wind up so far away. Where we sit right now? I couldn't be any farther away from home and still be in the continental U.S. You said 'barrel.'"

"What?"

"You said you looked down the barrel of the shotgun. Odd?"

"I said that?"

"You said barrel. So it wasn't a double-barrel?"

"No..., it was a single barrel shotgun."

"You can see that. Who do you see behind the shotgun?"

"Karl, maybe, I don't know."

"Maybe, but I doubt it."

"I doubt it too," he said.

"You gotta try to remember your secret lover."

"Please, Quinn, don't put it that way. I'm having a hard enough time here.... Can this possibly be happening? Am I trying to solve my own murder?"

And was I trying to help him? Da frick.

"Jeannie can't wait to give up her virginity. Her boyfriend, for whatever reasons... let's take him at his word... won't deliver. If she went to another boy, everybody would know it before the end of the seventh period. I think she'd go to an older man, someone who could teach her and keep his mouth shut."

"Yes," he said. "She used him, thinking that would be all right with him, with any older man. Have you ever used a man just for sex, Quinn?"

Why deny it, there were a lot of men in the late sixties, early seventies, just because I could. The right had finally been seized, including one memorable one-night stand with a Japanese akido instructor, but I had always had some mutual connection beneath the skin. Maybe not the things sonnets are made from, but nothing so simple as using someone to satisfy a need.

"No," I told him. "I never have."

"Being used, that could be a motive for murder."

"If he, you know, fell in love, or something. If he lost his mind."

"Like Houser," said Odd.

"Good example."

"She never expected that would happen. How could that happen? She thought she was choosing someone safe, someone older, someone who would walk away and keep his mouth shut, someone who would have to keep his mouth shut."

"Someone married?"

"Yes. Or a friend of the family... a teacher... someone who had something to lose if he talked about it."

"A teacher makes sense, married or not. If he's discovered, he loses his career. A teacher, because what was she after, really, besides knowledge? Carnal knowledge, the great mystery explored with a seasoned guide."

"Is that what you did?" he asked.

"I wish. Me and 'Our Johnny,' both of us stumbling terrified sixteen-year-olds in the back of his father's station wagon, scared to death. I didn't know it would hurt so much, when he started. After, the condom was wet when he took it off—duh?— and he made us both panic-stricken it had broken on us. Other than that, it wasn't half bad."

"What happened after that?"

"We didn't do it again for two months, and then we did it again, and after that we didn't do it anymore ever."

"We're all pretty stupid, aren't we? I mean, that first time."

"Then I don't want to be smart. At least there was passion, loss of control, eyes closed and labored breathing, sighs and cries and tingles, and I miss it all, I miss it so much—skin, sopping wetness, handfuls of tightly clutched ass."

Odd's head came forward, then turned toward me. I looked him right in the eye and confessed, "The last time

I got off was a date-rape with myself. That's when I gave it the nickname, 'Little Sahara.'"

11

The wipers were on intermittent because it started to drizzle again. The radio was off, the digital clock read 2:48. At the fireworks stands a slow but building trade was gathering.

We were on our way to the Tribal Headquarters, to check with Shining Pony on the condition of our boy Houser.

"I don't know what made me say all that, Odd."

"Maybe you thought we were having a girl gabfest," he said.

Sometimes you just have to laugh, ain't?

"Do you know why?" he asked me.

"Why what?"

"Why that suddenly happened to you."

"It wasn't all that sudden."

"You ought to know, Quinn, all the guys think you're pretty hot."

"All the guys...? I'm used up, buddy."

"That's not true. A woman doesn't get used up, I don't care what age she is. How old are you?"

"I'm forty-nine."

"Forty-nine. That's not even old. That's only... that's how old Jeannie would be if she lived."

"So she never knew what she was missing," I said, the bitch back in my voice.

"Forty-nine is not old, not even," he said.

"There's no reason in God's world for any man to come into me again."

"It's not God's world; it's yours." For Odd this bordered on irreverent outrage. For the moment, he was like the rest of us. "He may have made it but He doesn't live here any more. Quinn, I'm disappointed in you, man; you're a tough chick. I can't believe you're caving in like this."

Sweet boy, he didn't have a clue. He thought it was something I could fight. "It's got a name, Odd; it's called menopause, and the tough and the weak stand about the same chances against it, and, frankly, they ain't good."

"I know about menopause."

"Men don't know shit; why should they?"

"Well, that's pretty obvious. Every man has a woman, or wants one."

"So what do you know about menopause?"

"I know you stop having periods, you get hot flashes…"

He knew more than I gave him credit for. Hell, he knew more than I did when it hit me.

"Phantom sweats," I said, "so bad you want to rip off your clothes and run through the rain."

"You can do that; who's going to stop you?"

"Tell me what else you know."

"That you get used to it, that it passes, and if you were sexy before you can be sexy after. Look at Tina Turner!"

Could he have any idea how often *I have* looked at Tina Turner, wondering if at the end of the show she slips between silk sheets with a stud muffin half her age and fucks his brains out; or is it all performance, and her reality is that off the stage she sits weary and alone with a cup of tea praying he doesn't walk by and say something like, "Honey, you in the mood tonight?"

"No, look at me," I said. "My hair is brittle, I'm tired all the time, I'm getting fat; I'm going bitchy...."

"You always were bitchy."

"Fuck you."

"See?"

"This is real life. Tina Turner is a dream, a man's dream."

"I had a dream about you once," he said.

"I'm gonna slap you upside the head."

He laughed. "I did, really."

"What went on in this dream?"

"I can't tell you."

"Don't make me stop this car."

At least we were smiling, laughing a little. That's the only way to feel any better, ain't?

"There's got to be stuff you can take," he said, "some medicine."

"Oh, sure, there's stuff you can take. There's estrogen."

"There you go."

"But that boosts your odds for breast cancer. You can mix it with progestin, which really increases your chances. Or you can take testosterone."

"The male hormone?"

"That'll have you doing it again, like a mink. Only

problem is, you'll grow a beard, fart a lot, and beat the shit out of any guy who accidentally bumps into you."

"The beard thing could be a turn-off."

I was glad to see the little double-wide Tribal Police Headquarters loom into sight. We pulled up in front and went inside. Instead of Robert there was another young man behind the counter who looked a lot like Robert. He looked at us like he should know us but didn't.

"Can I help you?" he said.

"Chief in?"

"Chief!" he yelled to the back office. "Man and a woman, here."

"Send them back, Robert."

So it was another young man who looked like Robert and was also named Robert. Some island. We walked back to his little office. He was expecting to see us in uniform. He leaned forward on his chair, elbows to the desk, and looked us over, as though an unfamiliar pair like us could be trouble.

"You saw the Coyotes," he said.

"How'd you know, smoke signals?" I asked, and, of course, that was strike three on me.

"It's a small island."

"Not so small I'd want to back-hoe it into the water," I said, which is exactly what I would like to see someone else do. I was on a roll, and Odd had the good sense to throw himself in front of it.

"Do you mind?" he asked the chief. "We had time to kill and we can't resist a mystery."

Speak for yourself, Odd. I can't resist chocolate. A mystery can wither and fade away while I dunk for Godivas.

"It's a free country... except for the rez, where you answer to me. Which mystery is it you can't resist?"

"There's another?" I said.

"Old man Drinkwater is convinced Jeannie lives in your form," he said, looking at Odd.

"Has he convinced you?" Odd asked.

"No. I'm a Christian."

"Then we're back down to only one mystery: Who killed two kids on a rainy night so long past? Could it be Karl Gutshall?"

"You saw Karl?"

"We shook his chain," I said.

"Well put. The poor guy's been in a trap all these years. A lot of people still think he's guilty."

"You?"

"I don't know."

"We'll know," said Odd, "before we leave this island."

Under normal circumstances I don't rattle, but normal circumstances had flown some time back and what we were into now was paranormality at its spookiest. I was not used to anger in Odd, and I was not used to that resolute tone in his voice. Most of the time he could hold four opposing points of view simultaneously, which works against you as a cop. Often he seemed unsure of himself, of the path, and of the destination. Now I was impressed. And so was the chief, if not a bit worried about the steady equilibrium long enjoyed by his little island reservation.

I told him why we had dropped by, to see about the current health of our boy Houser. He got on the phone to his wife, speaking in Shalish, which I thought impolite, but considering my own mouth I could not object. I waited and watched his face for some reaction. Nada. He hung up and said, "Much improved."

We drove there in two cars, again. Odd was deep into himself and I left him wherever that was, wondering only about what Connors did for lunch and was he alone or with Esther. Did he bring a sandwich from home and eat it quickly in the break room, or did he and Esther go to Pizza Hut and urge the last piece upon each other?

We pulled up next to the chief's car in front of his house. The first thing I noticed was that Stacey and her mom had decamped from his front porch.

"Where's your wailing little friend?" I asked, when we got out of the car.

"Half way to Spokane, I hope," he said.

We followed him up the stairs to the room where they were keeping Houser. He was sitting up in bed, taking broth without assistance. The window was open and the cool air cleansed the sick room. He gave the empty bowl to Mrs. Shining Pony and thanked her. I asked her what his temperature was.

"Ninety-nine, point six," she said.

"That's not bad," I said.

"It's dropping."

She took his tray and left the room.

"How're you feeling, Houser?" I asked.

"Better," he said. "Much better. I thought I heard Stacey...."

"I wouldn't be surprised. I think they heard her in Bellingham."

"Is she still here?"

"She's a little girl, what do you care? She's with her mother, where she belongs."

"Houser...?" The patient turned to the sound of Odd's voice and found him sitting by the window. "How did it start? With Stacey."

"What do you mean?"

I interrupted. "Houser, do you remember me reading you your rights?"

"No."

"Then I'm gonna do it again," and I did, and we all waited until he told us he understood.

"You know we're cops, ain't? Him and me? From Spokane? And we'll be taking you back there for booking?"

He understood all that.

"All right, so if you want to talk to Odd, or anybody else, without a lawyer present, be my guest."

"What did you want?" asked Houser of Odd.

"I want to know how it started, with Stacey. She's fourteen, you're thirty-something. Did she come to you? Was she looking for a guide? A sexual guide? Was she a virgin at the time?"

"She still is," said Houser.

What?

12

I wondered if Houser was clever enough to be laying down a defense, that being that the crime in question never occurred. Or at least not the crime of penetration. But if that was the case, what was he doing with a fourteen-year-old girl clear across state on a little island hard against Canada? Nature walks? And besides, if he was lying, one quick peek with a professional eye would catch him.

"We were running away from rumors and hatred and intolerance."

Pul-leeze! He was running away from the law that keeps grown men out of the pants of little girls. I wanted to cover his face with the pillow, snuff the sucker out, but Odd was gentle with him, wanting to hear the whole story.

"How did you meet?" he asked.

"In church," said Houser.

I wanted to puke.

He was in the row behind her and across. She was sitting with her mother, and she kept turning to look at him, until their eyes met. He smiled at her, thinking no more than she was a teenager bored to death. She smiled back, a mischievous grin. They did things with their eyes, silent sarcastic commentary to whatever was going on in the Sunday ritual. He was there alone, a shaky believer, half out of habit, half out of fear. She was there because her mother dragged her along, though she shared some of the devotion, and a little of the fear. It was a harmless game they played, an adult and a child in an amusing conspiracy.

A week passed. He thought about her as he worked on computer systems. He was experienced with UNIX, AIX, HPUX, LINUX, all those things. He had a girlfriend, Clare, a tenured middle school Spanish teacher, who wanted to get married. She was twenty-nine and not at all unattractive, with rich red hair and a soft plump body and a sense of humor and a big heart and a good head on her shoulders. Houser was anxious that he would eventually marry her.

The next Sunday, in church, he changed his seat so that he better would be in that funny teen-age girl's line of vision and they could play their game of smiles and looks. Each Sunday after, he made sure to arrive just at the start of the processional hymn and to find a seat close to hers.

One Sunday, after the service, while her mother was chatting on the steps of the church with the pastor and Houser was standing at a distance watching, the girl came to him, and her walk was girlish and enchanting, and her yellow hair bounced in the breeze, and her lips curled in a conspiratorial grin, and all she said was, "Hi," and all he said back was, "Hi," and he was gone, in her control, captured by her youth and beauty and innocence. It was a moment he had never imagined and had no defenses against. He adored her.

Before long, she was visiting him at his apartment, in the evenings and on weekends, and that is where Clare discovered them together and was outraged, first confronting

Charles, who admitted he was powerless against the charms of this young girl, and soon after filing a report with the police. He was arrested and released on five-thousand dollars bail, put up by his parents. Stacey was at his apartment when he returned, telling him she could not live without him. They ran.

"But you had never had sex?" asked Odd.

"No."

"You were in love with her?" he asked.

"I was, I am, I always will be," he said.

"And she's in love with you?"

"She's much older than fourteen, in many ways," he said.

"Sure she is," said I. "People who are in love express it, physically. I mean, you can't help it, when you're in love."

Listen to me, expressing it physically. Like I knew.

"I know that," he said. "We kissed."

"You kissed?"

He looked at me like, what's wrong with that?

"A kiss is the glory of the universe," he said. "A kiss is the most beautiful and satisfying of all physical encounters. We kissed all the time. It was like food and drink to us."

I wanted to spit, but before I could work it up or aim it, Odd asked, "Did you teach her to kiss?"

"We taught each other."

"What's to learn?" said I.

"Oh, there's a world to learn."

"And... where did you kiss?" asked Odd.

"Everywhere."

"I mean, did you kiss her... toes?"

"Yes, her toes, all over, every part of each other, we kissed," said Houser, dreamily.

The chief, who had made himself wood, much like Odd had been trying to explain to me on the trip here, now showed signs of warping and cracking. I was getting a little bent out of shape myself. Kissing where?

"What would you say, Charles," said Odd, "if I told you that Stacey was only using you, that she has a boyfriend her own age, that what she won't do with you, she does with him, and that she isn't a virgin at all?"

What color the broth had brought to Houser's face now paled, and his hands started to shake, his teeth clamped down, and if he had not been weak and in bed I would swear that mild-mannered Charles Houser, half-believer in God and Heaven and Hell, was capable of murder at that moment.

This false scenario Odd used to provoke Houser might have been clever had Houser been guilty of anything more than he'd already confessed, but the ploy was thirty years too late and exercised upon the wrong suspect. He let Houser off the hook, explaining that the scenario was hypothetical. Stacey was still the essence of innocence, he supposed.

When we left the room and descended the stairs, the chief said in his solid even way, "Take that man back to Spokane." He was leading us down the stairs, first him, then Odd, then me, so we could not see his face. At the bottom of the stairs we formed a small circle and his face was the same.

We spoke in whispers. "It's your call, Quinn," said Odd.

I wanted nothing more than to get off that island, da frick. I looked outside to the porch and saw that the rain had come back, huge drops falling through the sunlight, and it looked so nice. It would be so nice to be driving through it, back to Spokane.

Odd needed to stay, I knew. If he went back to Spokane, took some vacation time, and returned, he might lose whatever was compelling him. We already had the cottage; we needed the rest. I decided there would be no harm in waiting until morning.

"He still has a fever," I said, "and he doesn't look all that great. I think a night's rest all around is the ticket. We'll take him back in the morning."

"You'll take him now," said the chief. "The Tribal Constitution allows me to hold non-tribal suspects for twenty-four hours. We've already passed that."

Any time a man cites the constitution, I wonder what he's got to hide, but that's me; I'm a cop. The chief never mentioned the twenty-four-hour rule before, and he didn't seem all that intimidated by defying the county when we first met him. Granted, he was never enthusiastic about the case that had fallen into his jurisdiction, but he clearly wasn't a guy focused on covering his ass. Or he would never have put the ailing felon in his own guest room. It's possible that the vision of Houser and that little girl licking each other from noses to toeses torched off a decent man's outrage and he simply wanted shed of him. It's also possible that our questioning the Coyotes and then Karl Gutshall infringed on some real or imagined territory sensitive to the chief.

I looked at my watch. It was a little after four. "What's another night?" I asked.

"That man is your prisoner," said the chief. "If you want him, take him. Otherwise, I'm turning him over to county, within the hour. Take him or lose him."

We took him.

Back up the stairs, this time just Odd and me. We had to wake up Houser. We helped him out of bed. He was in his boxer shorts, blue. We helped him into his clothes. He didn't object or question us. He had a bag, he said, that was in his car. We found it in the closet.

"Any weapons in that bag?" I asked.

"No, ma'am."

"Then you won't mind if I look through it?"

"No."

Just the usual stuff, clothes and toiletries. There was a CD player with two tiny attachable speakers and half a dozen CDs I didn't bother to look at. My music is no music. I zipped up the bag and handed it to Odd. We marched him down the stairs between us. The chief and his wife were standing at the foot of the stairs.

"Thank you, ma'am," said Houser, "for your hospitality."

She said nothing.

"You can catch the 4:45 ferry if you hurry," said the chief.

"Was it the smoke signals crack?" I asked, but the chief didn't answer. All he wanted was rid of us.

We threw Houser's bag in the trunk, and I took out a pair of cuffs. "Put your hands behind your back." I cuffed him and we made him comfy in the back seat. "I suppose we should stop somewhere and put on our uniforms," I said to Odd. He didn't answer. He didn't open up his door, even though the sky had darkened and it was starting to rain in earnest. "Ain't?"

"I can't go, Quinn," he said.

"Get in the car before you're soaked."

We got inside, but I didn't start the engine.

"You can take him back alone," said Odd. "This guy's no risk. You drove all the way here; you can drive all the way back."

"Yeah, I could do that. And the lieutenant would have a conniption, and you would be in the toilet, career-wise."

"I'll just have to deal with that."

"Let's say I spontaneously combust. Here's a prisoner sitting on the side of I-90."

"You're not going to spontaneously combust."

"Something bad, then. Same result. That's why they send two, buddy. You can't go over the hill on me. We got a responsibility in the backseat here?"

"If there's anything I can do...," said Houser.

"Shaddup."

"I've got to stay here," said Odd. "This is bigger than

me, or you, or this guy. How do I walk away and pretend it was… what? *Déjà vu?*"

I looked back at the prisoner. He was leaning forward, the better to hear, and he was dying to ask.

That knot in my stomach took its first loop when the chief told us to take Houser. It looped again going back up the stairs, and pulled tighter still putting him into the car. Anything other than taking the prisoner right back to Spokane was indefensible.

"How do we do anything else?" I asked Odd. "Look, this other thing has been hanging for thirty-some years; you expect to settle it overnight?"

"At least give me that, overnight. We were supposed to have that long anyway, and it was fine with the lieutenant. Let's stick to that."

"That was before we were saddled with the custody of kissy-face here. You wanna shoot him and dump him in the Sound so we can solve a murder?"

"Not *just* a murder, *my* murder!"

"I beg your pardon?" said the prisoner.

"Shaddup!" said I.

"We have to go to Jeannie's house. We have to talk to her parents. At least that much, we have to do. If nothing comes of that… if it doesn't convince you… then, the hell with it."

"Jeannie who?" asked Houser.

"Shut up, da frick!"

"'Frick'?"

"The lieutenant expects us to stay the night," said Odd.

"Didn't he even tell you not to check in unless you had to? He doesn't want to hear from us; all he wants is Houser when we bring him in, that's all."

"And what do we do with him in the meantime, take him to the Honeymoon Cottage, take him to Jeannie's house?"

"Who's Jeannie and why are we going to her house?"

"He's Jeannie!" I screamed, jabbing a finger at Odd. "He's Jeannie, all right? You understand now?"

Houser quietly slid back on the seat, as far away from me as he could get.

As we drove to the Tidewater Cottages I ran through my mind all the things that could go wrong, knowing they all would, and more besides, other things that I could not even anticipate. First of all, Frank and Angie. They see us leading a man in handcuffs into the Honeymoon Cottage and the whole island hears of the Spokane orgy. I drove past once, looking for them. The rain must have kept them indoors. It would also give us cover. I circled back and pulled up to our cottage, waited a moment for any welcome home committee, then turned off the ignition. Each of us grabbed a Houser elbow and hustled him up the porch and into the cottage.

Odd ran back to the car for Houser's bag. I sat the rapist, or whatever he was now, roughly on a wicker rocker and went to the bathroom for a towel. I toweled my hair and looked around at our little cottage. A light had been left on, turned low. The Bee Gees were on the stereo. The bed was high and fluffy and just big enough for two. The davvy had a blue floral pattern. The walls were crowded with framed dried flowers or watercolors of lush live ones. The carpet was well worn.

"This is nice," said Odd when he came back in and dropped Houser's bag. He unlocked the cuffs and removed them, saying, "Can I do this? I mean, are you going to try anything funny?"

"Me…?"

"Because I will shoot you, and it will stand, believe me."

"You don't even have a gun."

"I have a gun. It's in the car."

I sat on the cedar chest at the foot of the bed, the towel over my head. This one was a killer. I imagined I had steam rising from my hair, and my cheeks were full of glowing embers. Rivers of sweat ran over my ribs. I pushed off one shoe with the other, unlaced that one, pulled off my black service socks. I expected them to be dripping with sweat. They weren't, of course.

"… *I looked at the skies, running my hands over my eyes… and I fell out of bed, hurting my head, from things that I said…*"

"So let's see," said Houser, "I make a run for it, and you run out to your car and get your gun, and now I'm, what, a hundred yards away…?"

"I'll catch you; I'm faster than you."

"I've been sick."

"And then I'll shoot you."

"… *til I finally died, which started the whole world living, oh, if I'd only seen , that the joke was on me…*"

"You want to shoot me? Go ahead, I don't care. My life is ruined anyway."

"There's always the next one."

I threw off the towel. I might have said something; I might have screamed; I don't remember. My sweatshirt and T-shirt were off and flying by the time I hit the porch. I yanked off my new Wranglers. I pulled off my bra and passed it into the end zone, pulled down my panties and drop-kicked them for the extra point. Then I ran, ran through the pouring rain, over some gravel and didn't care, and into a stand of cedars.

Odd's voice kept calling, "Quinn, Quinn, Quinn! Wait!" I ran. Under the cedars the soil was spongy with rotting vegetation. Then I was on the muddy beach, slowed down by the mud, which was sucking down my feet. I was panting heavily. I stopped finally, spread out my arms, lifted up my face into the rain. I fell back on the mud and let the cold rain wash me down. I opened up my legs to it, I opened up Little Sahara to the downpour, but still I was arid there and on fire outside. I rolled over to my hands and knees, Connors' favorite position.

I could hear Odd's voice in the distance, "Quinn! Quinn!" Some clams just below the surface spit up arcing streams of juice, like miniature fire boats trying to put out the fire that I had become.

On my feet, I ran into the frigid salt water. I swam as far as I could, then realized I would have to swim back. I turned back to the beach and saw Odd standing there, waving my jeans and T-shirt over his head.

13

Naked and crazy, in deep icy salt water, I looked to the shore and my partner. I had to either swim back while I still could or drown. Odd stood at the water's edge, not knowing where to put his eyes. I came out of the brine not knowing where to put my hands. I was too cold and exhausted to care. I pressed my nakedness against him and he gave me his warmth, rubbing my back roughly with his big warm Swedish hands, bringing back the circulation. He had my jeans draped over his shoulder. He pulled my T-shirt over my head. Then he held me by one arm and helped me step into the jeans. He wrapped himself around me again and squeezed tight, and soon the numbing cold was gone and I had some feeling again. He didn't know what to ask and I didn't know how to explain it, and so he kissed me, full on the mouth. It was honest and comforting and I took it all.

"I'm sorry, Quinn. I'm way out of line."

"Forget it."

I didn't make a big deal of it. I made no deal at all of it.

"You ready to go back?" he asked.

I nodded. He took my arm like I had just had four wisdom teeth removed and he was walking me to the car. I did feel something had been removed, I just didn't know what.

We were halfway through the stand of cedars before a greater sense of reality took hold and I realized another actor should have been onstage.

"Odd... where's our prisoner?"

"I handcuffed him to the refrigerator door. Otherwise, I could have caught you before you took the plunge. Where did you think you were going, Canada?"

"Odd...? I wouldn't want anyone knowing about this."

He smiled his half-crooked smile. "I wouldn't either."

"Let's let it slide, all of it."

Going back across the gravel to the cottage, I felt every pebble under my bare feet. When you walk like that you tend to look at your feet, helping them along, which is why I didn't notice who was on the porch until I heard Odd's hoarse whisper, "Good night...," and I looked up to see Gwen, Stacey's mom, sitting on the step, her elbows on her knees, dragging deeply on a cigarette. My panties and bra were within range of the second-hand smoke, draped over a porch rail.

We knew it was her before she recognized us, dismissing us at first as another couple shacking up at the cottages. When she did realize who we were, her face turned apologetic. She tried to say something but couldn't get any traction between her mind and her mouth.

"What are you doing here?" asked Odd.

That didn't concern me as much as the whereabouts of her orally inclined daughter and our prisoner.

"God," she said, "I thought... it's you. You threw me. I was waiting for a couple of cops, and then... you guys...."

"Where's Stacey?" I said, all else put aside, except for my underwear, which I grabbed.

"Inside," she said. "You see, we...."

Neither one of us was interested in her explanation. We rushed by her and into the cottage. Thank God, Houser was still cuffed to the reefer, the door swinging open. Stacey was next to him, hips touching, leaning against the counter and drinking from a bottle of Molsons. When she realized it was us, she put the bottle down in front of her loverboy.

What a waste of a mad run naked through the rain and a baptism in the cold salty Strait. I was all outrage and business again, bent on keeping the peace and covering my ass.

"You," I spit at Stacey, "stand over here."

She looked like she'd love to make an issue of it, but it was my cottage, after all, and she was there uninvited. She obediently moved away from Houser.

"You didn't have to chain him like an animal," she said, needing not to let it go on my terms entirely.

Gwen had tossed her cigarette and now was behind Odd, who was behind me. "I can explain it," she said. Odd made her sit on the wicker. I made Stacey sit on the bed. We stood between them. Houser watched from his tether.

"You're soaking wet," said Gwen.

"Yeah, I know that."

"You should get out of your clothes and dry off before you catch a cold. We're in no rush."

"Oh, you're not in a rush. Thank you."

"Maybe you'd better," said Odd.

"Off," I said to Stacey, and when she stood up I tore off the bedspread and went into the bathroom.

I pulled off the wet T-shirt and the muddy jeans and toweled myself off. I wrapped myself in the bedspread and caught a glimpse of myself in the mirror. How do I explain all this to Connors, and do I leave out the kiss with a man thirty-one, -two, -three? A *naked* kiss, me anyhow. If I tell him it meant nothing, an unavoidable accident, will I free him up to make a similiar confession to me, using the same alibi? All it was was a kiss, though if Houser were an authority, and he might be, a kiss is the "glory of the universe." It was nice.

I longed for twenty-four hours ago when all I feared was losing my essence, and that had already happened.

"You aren't gonna believe this," said Odd, when I emerged from the bathroom.

"They got a litle laundromat here," said Gwen, jumping in nervously, "next to the boiler room. I could laundry your clothes for you. Between me and Stacey, we ought to have enough for you to put together a dry outfit. Our bags are over there, just help yourself."

"What are your bags doing in our cottage?" I asked, knowing that was part of what I wouldn't believe, according to Odd, who was smiling at me and the situation.

"They were on their way to the ferry," he said, "homeward bound. But...."

"But what?"

"Their car broke down."

"First time that ever happened," said Gwen. "Honda makes a dependable product, but that one does have a hundred 'n sixty thousand miles on it, and... I got it real cheap. There's this old boyfriend...."

"You don't have to tell them everything, Mom," said Stacey.

"Guess who gave them a tow?" said Odd. "Guess who's fixing their car?" said Odd.

"Karl Gutshall," said I, and he laughed. I didn't see what was so damned funny.

"*Trying* to fix it," said Gwen. "I gotta call tomorrow and get the damage."

"Tomorrow?"

"Beginning to see why they're here?" asked Odd.

"No, no...."

"This is the only place got rooms," said Gwen, "and they don't got any rooms, not that it matters much anyway, since my Visa is maxed out. Anyway, that nice old couple told us you had this place and we should talk to you."

"Why in the world would you feel we're obliged to take you in?" I asked Gwen.

"I was kind of hopin' Spokaneans would stick together," she said.

"We don't even like Spokane... or Spokaneans."

Odd laughed. I went to the reefer, pushed Houser aside and got a Molsons. I popped the top and took some down.

"That can't be true," said Gwen. "Otherwise, you wouldn't be cops there, takin' an oath and everything."

"By this time tomorrow we probably won't be cops."

"Oh, sure you will, 'cause we're all gonna cooperate. Now, listen, I'm a good cook," argued Gwen. "I could make us a nice dinner here. And don't think that I would want to take your bed away from you, you two can have that...."

"We're partners," I said, "we don't sleep together; doesn't anybody understand that?"

"Well, whatever.... I only meant, we can work something out; it's just for the one night."

"This man is our prisoner," I tried to explain. "He will be charged with statutory rape, and that one," nodding toward Stacey, "is his victim...."

"I'm not a victim!" she hissed. "How can you charge him with anything if there's no victim? You think I'll testify? *As if!*"

"... and whatever his sentence turns out to be," I continued, ignoring her for the moment, because it would be impossible to ignore her for much longer, "it will include the order to never again come in contact with her."

"Try and stop us," said Stacey.

"And you expect me, as an officer of the law, to allow a rapist and his victim to share the same room for an overnighter? I don't think so."

"I'm not a rapist," whispered Houser, ashamed.

Stacey was too outraged to spit, that I should label their love with such crass and negative name-calling. I got all that from her eyes, and in spite of myself I envied the passion I saw in them.

"I don't think anyone would fault us, Quinn, considering the circumstances. We can let Houser sleep on the kitchen floor, cuffed. Gwen and Stacey can have the bed, you can sleep on the sofa, and I'll sit on the rocker with my weapon in hand. Anyone tries anything, I'll shoot them."

"You're just dying to shoot someone, aren't you?" said Houser.

Odd smiled.

"Are you enjoying this?" I asked.

"Compared to everything else," he said, "it's a relief."

14

Odd drove to the little island grocery store and persuaded them to stay open a few minutes longer so that he could buy the things on Gwen's shopping list. They stayed open even longer, long enough to tell him what they remembered, that Jeannie was a rare beauty, jewel of the island. Everybody had a crush on her, but there was one particular boy, only twelve, who followed her around like a puppy. Who? They couldn't remember. They remembered only that for a time he was her shadow.

Gwen, true to her word, gathered up my clothes and some of their own and took them to the laundromat. I was left with Houser and Stacey and my second bottle of Molsons. I moved Houser from the reefer to the rocker and cuffed him to the arm of it. He was no great risk and I was thinking seriously of bagging the cuffs, but the presence of Stacey made me uneasy. Individually, they were harmless. Together, I didn't want to know.

I made her stay on the bed and the inactivity was driving her nuts.

"No TV in this dump, no magazines even. Charlie, don't this suck?"

"Don't talk to him," I ordered.

"I can't talk to him?"

"What did I just say?"

"Well, then, can I talk to you?"

"Only if you have something big to say?"

"How do I know if it's big?"

"If you don't know, don't say it?"

She was in bare feet. She yanked at a ragged toenail, then said, "Your boyfriend's a real babe."

"He's not my boyfriend, and that wasn't a big thing to say."

"You have to tell Charlie not to get jealous 'cause he gets jealous when I say somebody else is a babe, even though I might be teasing. Your guy really is, though. What's his name?"

"None of your business."

"Jeez, don't you ever chill out?"

"No."

"I'd just as soon hitchhike home as be stuck here with you, Lady."

"I'd just as soon you did that too."

"Girls, girls...," said Houser. "Can't we all just get along?"

She was a spirited girl, I'll give her that, and I wondered what she saw in Houser. My mother always used to say there's a lid for every pot. Even she would have to admit some matches are better left unmade. I had to remind myself this was neither a match nor a mismatch; it was a felony.

"I don't know why you guys are staying here anyway," she said. "If you came here to bust Charlie, what's holding you back?"

I took one of the bar stools from the other side of the counter and brought it around to my side, in the kitchen proper, and sat down. I drank my Molson's. I planned to hit her over the head with the empty when I finished.

"They've got something else going," said Houser.

"Shaddup."

"You are so rude," said Stacey.

"They're working on some murder case, and that's why they have to stay 'til tomorrow."

"Really? Cool! Who got murdered?"

"Her partner. Odd."

"That's pretty odd, all right, because the dude is still alive."

I was too tired to shut them up. I wanted to push her off the bed, lie down, and sleep for about a year.

"Odd is the dude's name. Now. But it used to be Jeannie, and as near as I can tell, that's who got murdered."

Stacey was unable to grasp it. Join the crowd. My head got heavy, and down it went, click by click, into my folded arms on the counter. She said something, and he said something back, but it sounded far away, and I could care less, if I cared at all, which I didn't. I was out.

It could have been a minute; it could have been an hour. Let's say longer than a minute, because what woke me up was Gwen crying out, "Stacey!" She was standing in the doorway, her arms full of freshly laundered clothes. Her fourteen-year-old daughter was on her knees in front of the wicker rocker, her blonde head bobbing rhythmically between Houser's legs. Startled at the sudden appearance of her mother and my awakening, she bounded back into bed, wiping her mouth with the bottom of her T-shirt. She wasn't wearing any bra. Houser, one-handed, struggled to stuff his glistening and quivering thing back into his pants and zip up. It was not a pretty sight.

Gwen, defeated all over again, dropped the clothes on the foot of the bed and started sorting, shaking her muddled head in unhappy disbelief.

I don't know if it was the mother in me or the menopausal madwoman. It sure wasn't the cop. I kicked the bar-stool out from under me and I was on that bed in a nanosecond. The bedspread fell off me and for the second time in one afternoon I was publicly naked. Stacey fought back and cursed, but she was no match for me. There are druggies on Sprague Street who would rather be brought down by a canine officer than by me.

I pinned her arms behind her and got her over my knees and gave her the mother of all spankings. She regressed from a garbage-mouthed teenager to a spastic pre-pubescent, to one of the terrible two's, to a whimpering infant. Somewhere along that reverse psychic catapult she promised me the largest lawsuit known to man and the sure end to my career as a police officer. I could care less.

I retrieved my wrap and pulled it around me. Nobody said a word. The only sound now was Stacey's sniffling. Gwen had the shadow of a grateful look. Houser was aghast and maybe a little scared that I'd now get to him, which I might have, except my fury was spent, and he was, after all, a man manacled to a rocking chair. He didn't go to her; she came to him. All right, he was supposed to say no, but he's only a man and they're all dogs. I gave him the old one-two with my eyes. That was enough.

By then, Odd pulled up in the car. I decided not to burden him with a briefing of what had happened in his absence. No one else was eager to tell him. That way, at the hearing, he could deny all knowledge, etcetera.

He came inside, a grocery bag in one arm, and said, "Guess what, Quinn? There was a twelve-year-old boy used to follow Jeannie everywhere. He was in love with her."

Traumatized, Stacey was half-asleep, still sniffling. Houser slowly rocked, his chin on his chest. Gwen folded clothes automatically. I took my freshly laundered jeans, T-shirt, underwear, and socks, and went into the bathroom. Through the door I could hear Odd ask, probably to Houser, "What's wrong with her?" He could have been asking about any one of the three females under that roof.

I turned on the blower so that I wouldn't hear them talk and they couldn't hear me pee.

Gwen's claim to being a good cook was more or less true, though I suspected her range was narrow. The scope of her recipes, I mean, not the stove she cooked on. We had mac 'n cheese with little cut-up smoked sausages inside, the top nicely browned and crusty, and a cucumber and sour cream salad. My mother used to do the same meal and serve it with her homebrewed iced tea in the summers. Here, I had another Molsons. We sat at a little round dinnette, and Odd had to go get a couple folding chairs from Frank. He had been gone awhile for that and I knew he was pursuing his case, which I had all but forgotten since my spontaneous combustion earlier.

Gwen put on some of the CDs from Houser's bag and we all sat down to dinner. Before digging in, we joined hands and Stacey, as the youngest, said grace while we bowed our heads. Houser was on my right, his left hand cuffed to the chair, so I reached down and took the cuffed hand.

It was a grim little dinner at first, but the homey hot mac and the refreshing cool cuke salad soon restored us and before long we were like a family with issues that might never be resolved but at least could be put on hold long enough to get through dinner.

"The secret," said Gwen, "is the Velveeta. I've tried Tillamook but the good cheddars don't bind the mac like Velveeta."

I mumbled some words of interest, like the world is full of wonders, and why shouldn't Velveeta turn out to be one of them. I did not want to shut down any semblance of normality, but on the other hand I did not want to encourage more stupid talk. I asked Gwen what she did for a living, single parent and all that.

"I work construction," she said.

"Really?" She didn't look the type, woman in a man's world. I was the type.

"Highway construction. I'm the one with the orange vest and hardhat and the two-sided sign, stop and slow. I either wave you through or make you stop and wait."

"Is that a good job?"

"When it's not raining or freezing or scorching hot or you're almost taken out by some driver in too big a hurry, talking on their cell phone and all. It pays the rent; but to tell you the truth, all I ever wanted to be was a homemaker."

"Mother," whispered Stacey, a warning.

"But you need the right partner for that job," she went on, "and I could never quite swing it. Tried it three times. Stacey's father was number two. He was a long-distance hauler who one day just couldn't find his way back."

"Do you always have to tell everybody every lousy detail, Mom?" said Stacey. "Couldn't you just chill out?"

"The last husband was working out okay 'til he started getting fresh with Stacey."

"Mom!"

"Well, it's true!"

"That's all right, Gwen," I said, "you don't have to talk anymore."

I knew she felt obliged. She'd washed our clothes, made our dinner, and now thought she had to fill the dead air so that the imposition of her and her virgin daughter might be made a tad more palatable.

I changed the subject and asked Odd what the other incurable romantics had to say.

"Who?

"Frank and Angie."

"About what?"

"You know what. You were gone a long time for a couple of folding chairs."

"They told me that Jeannie's father is dead. He died a few years after, of a broken heart, everyone says. So it's just the mother. She lives not far from here, in the same house."

"Everything is not far from here; we're on an island. Everything but the world."

At the mention of Jeannie, both Stacey and Houser perked up. They looked at each other, in the know.

"I think I must have missed part of the conversation," said Gwen.

"You miss most of everything," said Stacey, and in the know of that was the real heartbreak.

"Respect your mother," I said. I knew she was right, though, and I knew what had been missed.

"I don't want to be presumptuous...," said Houser, and everybody at the table looked at him. For a moment I thought the attention would render him powerless to go on. Then he said, "... but maybe we can help. Five heads are better than two. And I'm trained in the analytical process."

"What?" asked Gwen. "What's going on?"

"Somebody got murdered, okay?" said Stacey. "It doesn't concern you."

Gwen's fork stopped on the way to her mouth.

"Don't worry; it happened a long time ago," I said.

"Who?" she asked.

Odd and I looked into our plates.

Houser nodded in Odd's direction and said, "Him."

The fork in Gwen's hand started to shake. Pieces of mac 'n cheese fell back to her plate. She laid down the fork and folded her hands in her lap.

"I don't understand," she said. "I don't understand anything."

I brought them all up to speed. I don't know why. Maybe because arrangements would eventually have to be made, and we were a group now, whether we liked it or not.

I expected some skepticism. I would not have been surprised by derisive laughter. Instead, all three of them gave my news the most serious kind of attention. Not that any of them, or either of us, for that matter, knew any more about past lives than what we had seen on TV talk shows: middle-aged women claiming to have been Cleopatra or Marie Antoinette. Or phoney channelers talking in fake voices to ancient masters, for a fee. Or psychics who could make that long distance call for you to your dearly departed, if the price was right. I never saw a psychic yet who could tell you what the weather would be like two weeks down the road.

Nobody jumped on that end of it, though. It was the double-murder itself got to them. If Odd had an inside track, and it seemed very much that he did, then he had to go with it, take it to the end, and bring down the son-of-a-bitch who blew away those two kids. On that, there was consensus, with one possible hold-out, me.

Stacey, especially, got into it, identifying with Jeannie, and confirming from her own raging hormones that Odd was surely right in his belief that it was an older man, and that the motive was jealousy.

"Here's the thing," she said. "If she hooked up with some other guy, she told somebody. You have to; you can't keep a thing like that to yourself."

"You told somebody... about us?" asked Houser

"Duh. I told Britney. I tell Britney everything."

"I told you not to tell anyone. You promised you wouldn't tell anyone."

"Anyone but Britney. You didn't tell anybody?"

"No," said Houser, "are you crazy?"

"Well... well... Britney saw me writing your name in my secret notebook and she made me tell."

"You wrote my name?"

"A thousand times," she said. "I loved you."

Houser looked like a man contemplating suicide by mac 'n cheese asphyxiation.

"Odd," I said, "you mentioned a secret notebook."

"I did?"

"When we were talking to Karl Gutshall. You said he tried to break into your... into Jeannie's locker and read her secret notebook."

"I don't remember that."

Joan Osborne was singing... about God, of all things.

"Do all young girls keep secret notebooks?" Odd asked Stacey.

"For sure," she said.

"I wish I'd known that," said Houser.

"Did you?" asked Odd, of me. "Keep a secret note-book?"

I could still see it, after all these years, pink, full of swirls, in each swirl a dream; but those I did not remember, not the dreams, just the swirls, so many of them.

"Even I did," said Gwen.

"Mom, please," said Stacey.

"Well, I did. I'm not going to tell you what was in it. That's for me to know and nobody to find out."

"If she boinked the guy who killed her," said Stacey, "she told someone. Word. And the name of the guy is written in her secret notebook. If that notebook is still around...."

"What if God was one of us... just a slob like one of us... just a stranger on the bus... tryin' to make his way home..."

I pushed my chair back and hurried outside to the porch. I hoped not to go crazy again. I hoped not to run into the sea. I hoped not to do that ever again. I went to the end of the overhang and cried into my hands like a lost little girl. Odd came out and stood next to me. He put his arm around my jerky shoulders and gave me a hard squeeze. He was a big Swede, six-two, -three.

"I miss the tough little broad I used to be," I said.

"Oh, you were never all that tough," he said.

"Tougher 'n this."

"That song always makes me cry, too."

I managed a chuckle. He was a funny kid, that Swede.

"You shouldn't have left those two alone," I said. "She'll be on her knees under the table."

"Her mother's watching her."

"Yeah, well, she's been doing a great job so far."

"I still have to go to Jeannie's house," he said.

I nodded. "I have to go with you."

"You don't, really. You can stay with the prisoner."

"Hell, let's just bring him along."

"What about the other two?"

"Not our problem. They can eat shit and die."

"Ah, you're back."

Gwen, as it turned out, was content to sit in the cottage but Stacey put up a fight, insisting that she could help with this. She petitioned us up to the car door, where we locked Houser in back and shut her out. She hopped gingerly on bare feet on the gravel as Odd backed the car around, still trying to worm her way along. We left her there.

We passed The Cedar Farm, where they sold siding and decking and other stuff made out of cedar. We saw three, four beater cars parked with *For Sale* signs on them. We took a left on Early Dawn Street, a right on Pullorbedamned Road, and another left on Sunset Boulevard. Odd seemed to know where he was going, God knows I didn't. We passed a place that sold topsoil and a place that sold gravel, and every place like that we passed was making me homesick. Not for Spokane, for Shenandoah, where they also struggled to survive on dirt and stone, and where I knew the lingo and everyone settled for just one life and the reward that was promised to follow.

Out of nowhere, Odd said, "The house is white," in a flat voice. "There is a screened-in porch. With an iron glider and a thick pad on it. On really hot summer nights you could sleep on that. In the back there's a deck where you can watch the deer. She always planted a little patch for them."

"Who?"

"The woman who lives there. It was a deal she made with them, with the deer. Eat out of your own patch and leave our garden alone. It seemed to work."

Da frick.

"She'll offer us cocoa," he said.

"Cocoa? Who drinks cocoa?"

"She'll be embarrassed that the house isn't cleaner."

"I know I always am. Where will the secret notebook be?"

"In Jeannie's room?"

"You asking me?"

"Unless she burned it."

"She wouldn't do that," said Houser, who had kept quiet up until then.

"No, I don't think so either," I said.

We entered a cedar-lined street of old wood-framed houses, and Odd pulled into a driveway without hesitation. The house was white, as he said it would be. There was a screened-in porch. Odd got out of the car like a sleepwalker. I locked the doors and ordered Houser to sit tight.

Inside the house, the lights were on. We opened the screen door to the porch. An iron glider was at the far end, as Odd said it would be. He was taking everything in. I rapped smartly on the door. A small dog barked. In a minute a woman cautiously opened the door a crack. Her hair was a rich natural white.

We held out our ID's and I told her who we were and where we had come from. Her eyes knitted up in confusion. Odd was in some sort of rapture. "Do you think we might talk to you for a little while?" I asked.

"What is it about?" she asked.

"About what happened long ago."

"About Jeannie? Why would the Spokane police...?"

"They wouldn't," I said. "It's us. Odd here, really. Could we come inside? It's complicated."

She looked at Odd, and I thought she looked at him with some kind of recognition.

"Yes, of course. I'm sorry. I'm a little...."

"I understand. You weren't expecting this."

"No... I wasn't."

She opened the door wide, holding back a little black-and-white terrier. We went into her house.

"You caught me by surprise," she said. "The house is a mess."

"Are you kidding?" I said. "You should see mine. You've got a lovely house here."

"Thank you. Please, sit down."

She sat on the edge of the settee, a little nervous and with some difficulty. She was in her early seventies and might have had some ostioporosis, but her eyes were bright and she had a healthy complexion.

Odd sat in a wide-armed, tattered, overstuffed chair, which had to have been the favorite of the man of the house, now deceased, and he smiled a broad smile that neither he nor any of his Swedish forebearers had ever even known was possible. Had I seen it on the streets of Spokane I would have thought someone was trying to start something.

He was home again.

The old lady smiled back at him.

The terrier jumped up on Odd's lap and snuggled in.

"Oh, Otis," she admonished the dog. "Just shoo him if he bothers you."

"It's all right."

"Dogs like him," I said.

"Some people have that," said she. "Jeannie was that way, dogs, cats, fawns…. Would you like some cocoa?"

"Maybe later," said Odd.

Do the math. He had it all right, batting a thousand.

"Well, then…." She waited for us to explain ourselves, but Odd seemed content just to sit and look at her. I would have to start the ball rolling, and of all places to start, I don't know what possessed me to ask, "Mrs. Olson, did your daughter Jeannie ever have trouble sleeping?"

It startled her.

"Yes, especially the last few years…. We were worried about it. When she was twelve she started thrashing in her sleep. Her bed in the morning was a tangle of sheets and blankets. But she never seemed aware of it when she awoke, so I thought maybe she was going through a growth spurt or something and it would pass. It was about the time her periods started."

"Really?"

"Why in the world do you ask?"

"If you could just indulge us…."

"I really don't understand why you're here," she said.

I told her, in broad strokes, why we had come to Shalish Island, and how we came to stay longer than we had anticipated. How Odd was drawn to the picture of Jeannie and James on the wall of the tribal police headquarters, and how one question led to another until we began, that is, Odd began to have certain insights into what might have occurred, that is, details about how it occurred. I didn't tell her what those details were, or how he came to have insight into them, or that we had a perp and a perv outside in our car. I had to leave something for Odd to tell her.

"Daddy took it hard, didn't he?" Odd asked her.

"Daddy?"

"Jeannie's daddy. He took it very hard."

"He was the third victim of that, really," she said. "Every evening he would wash the car, treat the rubber, the leather, polish the chrome... every evening. It's all he could do. It was a '65 Mustang that he had planned to give to Jeannie for her graduation, that she could take with her to college. Then he would pull it into the garage and hose down the driveway until not a leaf or a pebble or a twig remained. We had the only spotless driveway on the island. One evening after he did all that, he sat down on the wet driveway and died."

"I'm sorry he had to go through so much suffering," said Odd. "But it's over now."

"Yes, yes, it is."

"Jimmy's parents think Karl Gutshall is responsible," I said.

"I know they do, but I just can't imagine Karl doing such a thing. He was broken hearted when Jeannie broke up with him, yes, but he would never hurt her like that. If you ask me, he's another victim."

"Do you have any ideas who might have done it?" I asked.

"No, none at all. Everyone just loved to be in her presence. She had a glow that everyone wanted to be within. This island has never been the same without her, and that's not just because I was her mother."

"Yes," I said, "we've heard how special she was, the effect she had on people."

"You know," said Odd. "I think I'd like that cocoa now."

We followed her into the kitchen, and as she made the cocoa, Odd's eyes travelled over the counter, the table, the stove, and all the appliances.

He opened the door to a counter-top toaster-oven. "This is new," he said.

"That? No, it's ten years old if it's a day."

We talked about that terrible night. I was pretty much convinced by now that this lady was Odd's mother in another life. I surrendered; I accepted it; I waited to see where it would take us. We sat down at the kitchen table and drank the cocoa, which felt thick in my mouth.

"Mrs. Olson... can I call you by your first name?" I asked.

"Yes, of course you can."

"What is it, your name?"

"Janet," said Odd, simply, and sipped his cocoa, a long-lost man with his big hands around a familiar mug, an affectionate dog sleeping on his lap.

"Yes, that's right, my name is Janet."

"We're not here, Janet," I said, "in any official capacity, but this is more than a matter of curiosity to us."

"Do you… have some idea… who did it?" she asked, tentatively.

"No, but it may be possible now to find out."

"But how? It's been thirty-three years."

"Well… we might have an eye witness," I said.

"What? After all these years…?"

"There was a twelve-year-old boy had a crush on Jeannie," said Odd.

"Oh, all the boys had a crush on Jeannie. Did he see it, this boy?"

"He might have," said Odd.

"But that's not the eye witness we have in mind," I said. I wanted the other shoe to drop, and drop soon, but I didn't want to freak her out.

"He was a serious little guy," said Odd, "followed her around all the time, too afraid to talk. Jeannie towered over him."

"Gosh, it could have been anybody." She thought for a while and said, "I do remember… a little Indian boy."

"Yes! It was an Indian boy, a very shy boy, and Jeannie was the first girl he ever felt that way about. Do you remember his name?"

"Lord, it was so long ago. Maybe it will come to me.

But how do you know about that?"

"Ah, Janet, yes, that's the hard part to explain," I said, wishing Odd would take a crack at it and get it over with.

"Her room...," said Odd, "first door on the right at the top of the stairs. What's in there now?"

"It's still her room. We had no other use for it. We had no other children."

She was speaking reasonably, but I could see in her face a new level of confusion and fear, and she looked only at Odd, who casually scratched the terrier's neck.

"Could we see her room?" I asked.

She led us upstairs. The doors were all open. A sewing room at the top of the stairs, the master bedroom and the bathroom to the left, and Jeannie's room to the right. She went in ahead of us, and Odd seemed to falter at the last step, then regained himself and went into the room. It was a small room, with windows to the street. The bed was nicely made and populated with several stuffed animals. The dresser was maple and tucked into the mirror's framing were yellowing photos that once meant something to a young girl. A cedar chest was at the foot of the bed. On the floor was an old-style hi-fi set and on either side of it stacks of vinyl albums. There was a small bookcase with high school mementos placed among the books. In the far corner of the room was a door, which I assumed was the closet.

I took it all in, in just a second, and focused on Odd's face, looking for the flash of recognition. I believe Janet

Olson was doing the same thing. We were both waiting for him to say something.

"It's small," he said. The remark was anticlimatic. But I remembered the first time I went back home to Pennsylvania after many years on the west coast and went into my old room. My reaction was exactly the same. It seemed so much smaller than I remembered it.

Odd began looking closer, especially at the things in the bookcase, and he said, "There was a blue spiral notebook that she always kept with her, with stick-on's, all kinds of little goofy things the girls were sticking on their notebooks—the peace symbol, the Beatles, psychedelic flowers.... Do you know where that is?"

"The police came in and took all of that stuff," she said. "After a time, when no one was arrested, they returned it all, but I don't remember any blue notebook like that."

"It would have been here," he insisted. "Her name was on the cover... *Jeannie*... written in silver ink with great flourishes. And at the bottom, in black letters: *PRIVATE PROPERTY.*"

"Then you must have seen this notebook," she said. "Where?"

"That's the hard part," I said. "That might require more than cocoa."

Odd heard neither one of us. He was concentrating on that notebook, trying to reproduce it in his mind. He shut his eyes. "It was half diary, half junk heap," he said, "a doodle pad, a safe place for all her lists, all the things she wanted, all the things she wanted to do, to become, all the places she wanted to go, all her likes and dislikes, all her fears and dreams, everything. It would have been here. She took it to school with her every day and she brought it home after."

"Go to the last pages of the notebook," I whispered. "What is written there?"

The old woman backed away from us, into the doorway, ready to make what escape she could. She was trembling now, holding onto the door frame.

"In big letters...," said Odd. He lowered his head and searched through closed eyes.

I tried to help him along. "Yes, in big letters," I said. "Are they printed or cursive?"

"Both... big and small... printed and hand written. A name...."

"Yes," I said, "what is the name?"

He moved his head slowly, side to side, taking in the name he could now read in his mind.

"Ron," he said. "The name is Ron... and later... now it's James... pages of Ron, then pages of James...."

"Was there a boy named Ron in Jeannie's class?" I asked the old woman.

"Ron? No, none that I remember. None in the school, that I know of, and I knew all the kids."

"Where is the notebook?" I asked Odd.

"In my hands!"

"No, where now?"

He opened his eyes, turned to me and to Janet. "I don't know," he said.

"Are you a psychic?" she asked.

"I wish," said I.

Janet, still trembling, continued to hold onto the door frame. She was breathing heavily. "I remember now who it was," she said. "The twelve-year-old boy who was so infatuated with Jeannie."

15

The old woman had a ritual of making herself a martini at sunset, but only when there was a sunset to be seen, which kept her from having a daily drink, although it is strange how many times, she told us, how at the end of a dark gray day the horizon will open up and the sun will come out just long enough to set, providing spectacular contrasts, dark sky above, dying sun below, and then the green-blue water.

She mixed up a pitcher of martinis, Kettle One vodka. It was ten o'clock, and if there had been a sunset that evening, this far north, we would have been only minutes behind it.

I've seen black tar addicts start cooking with less anticipation than Janet prepping her martinis.

"You kept up the ritual," said Odd.

The long spoon in her hand stirred faster and faster.

"You and Daddy and your martinis at sunset," he said.

At last. There went the spoon, into the pitcher, and the woman looked liked she might dive in after. Odd went to her and took her into his arms. and she whimpered, "Oh, my God... oh, my God...."

"A mother knows," said Odd. "Doesn't she?"

The old woman nodded against his chest, then said hoarsely, "Yes, a mother knows."

He comforted her in his arms for a long moment. I salivated at the martini pitcher, worried that the ice would melt. I took it upon myself to pour.

"I have so many questions," she said.

"Me too," he said, "and very few answers."

"Yeah, well, I got a question of my own," I said, handing them each a martini. Screw the olives. "Who's the lovesick kid?"

"First a toast," said Odd. "You can't drink a martini without a toast. To the three of us."

I thought he meant the three of us standing there together, fine, but she started weeping again, and I knew he had echoed the toast her husband always made at sunset, to the three of them, father, mother, and daughter, the family.

"Wherever he may be," Odd added, "because he lives, somewhere."

It gave her strength, enough to hoist the glass, anyway. Color rushed back to her face, fueled by the powerful mixture of alcohol and essence of wormwood.

"It was Seth Shining Pony," she said, "the little boy who followed Jeannie around, the lovesick little boy."

"It was!" said Odd, smiling. "How could I not remember? He was an adorable little pest. If I smiled at him, or talked to him, he'd run away. Next day, he'd be back, following me."

Was it the drink or my hormone-starved body? Did it matter? I was sweating like a Fourth of July parade. It was Odd, good old Odd, the big Swede, macho man, solid as a stone, his own deep voice but speaking with the cadence of a teen-aged girl.

The memory he was reliving may have been flattering, it may have been amusing, but I were still a cop, and if I were going to be sucked into this, I would have to start thinking like one again. Who's the perp?

We found our way to the soft chairs for the second martini. On top of the beers I had earlier, I had a viable buzz stacking.

"Is a twelve-year-old capable of blasting two people with a shotgun?" I asked, a rhetorical question these days. There is hard evidence that the contemporary twelve-year-old can pull it off and go home to his PlayStation. But in 1967 American children had not yet turned that dark corner. Even in their fantasies, back in '67, they were still more suicidal than homicidal, Then something changed, who knows what?

"Seth is widely respected on the island," said Janet. "He's known to be a decent fair man."

"But what kind of kid was he?"

"I never heard anything bad about him."

"Okay. So he's rehabilitated," I said. "Most murderers are rehabilitated as soon as they're caught… or right after they've done the deed, meaning, they'll never do it again."

Odd was nursing his drink, thinking about it.

"He could have stolen that notebook," I said. "A twelve-year-old shadow, he would have had the opportunity. Odd?"

"I don't know. I can't remember."

"A great change came over the chief right after we talked to James' parents. He didn't like it. That's when he wanted us off the island."

"Then why did he cooperate with me originally? He took me to the crime scene; he didn't hide anything."

"Why should he? Look at us. Sherlock Holmes and Watson we ain't. He didn't have any reason to fear either one of us until we went to the Coyotes and the old guy started spreading it around that you... used to live here, in another body. Then it was, don't be late for the ferry."

"I don't know," said Odd. "Maybe he was so disgusted with Houser he just wanted him out of his house and off his island. We had nothing to do with it."

Houser! I'd forgotten all about him.

"Jeez Louise," I said, "Houser. Do you think he's still in the car?"

"I don't much care," said Odd.

But to me, the thought was sobering, messing up my nice buzz. I had visions of Stacey finding him, stealing our car, making a getaway, us losing our jobs. My paranoia cut short what could have been an all-nighter. Mrs. Olson didn't want Odd to go. He was, after all, the spirit of her daughter. And Odd would have been happy to stay. I finally convinced him it would be a good idea to drop in on the chief again, before it got too late.

"Yes, I would like to see the chief again," he said.

"But you'll come back, won't you?" she asked.

"Yes, I will."

"And stay for a while... I know you have a life in Spokane, but if you could spend some time here..."

"I would like that," he said, "if it's not too upsetting."

"Oh, I'll take that risk."

Enough had gone on in that house to spook a normal cop; but once outside, my immediate concern was, I don't see Houser. Like when you leave your dog in the parking lot while you pop into Walmart and you come back out and you don't see the mutt until you're right at the window, and he's hunkered down on the floor, sleeping, and you were already working out in your head how you would explain it to your husband that you lost the family pet. It was like that. Houser was curled up in the back seat, fast asleep. I let Odd drive.

"Did you find the notebook?" Houser asked.

"Shaddup," said I.

"C'mon, what happened?"

We ignored the perv.

We pulled up to the tribal police double-wide and went inside, this time dragging Houser along with us. Like when, after the Walmart thing you still have to stop at the bank but this time you bring Fido in with you because you're afraid of the way you thought you lost him, and at least here they'll give him a biscuit.

Robert was on duty, the first Robert. Though he looked a lot like the second Robert, I could tell the difference.

"Good evening, Robert," I said, best of friends. I was a little drunk. "The chief here?"

"Nope." He looked over Houser, trying to figure that one out.

"Hey, Robert," said Odd. "Where's your evidence locker?"

"Our what?"

"Your evidence locker," he said. "Where you keep evidence of crimes?"

"Why d' you want to see that?"

"Just a thought," said Odd.

"Hold on a second," the kid said, and he went into the back room.

"It's after eleven," I said. "What made us think the chief would be here?"

"He'll be here," said Odd.

"You think the notebook might be in the evidence locker?"

"Most likely not."

I was holding Houser by the back of his belt. He had nothing to say.

Robert came back out carrying a cardboard box with a lid on it, the kind of box made for storing files. He put it on the counter and took off the lid. It was their evidence locker.

We both stuck our heads over the counter and looked inside. Tagged hunting knives and a cheap .22 revolver, a broken longnecked Bud bottle with dried blood on the business end of it, a half-full pint of Kessler's, a baggie of grass, a set of skeleton keys, some phoney drivers licenses, and one disconcerting glass eye which seemed to look at us accusingly.

"What are you looking for?" we heard behind us. The chief, of course.

We turned but we didn't say anything, enjoying a little stare-down instead.

"Your prisoner looks healthy," he said finally.

"I wouldn't go that far," said I. "But we'll let a psychiatrist decide."

"Why are you still on the island, and what are you doing here?" he asked. A threat had entered his voice. Da frick.

"They wanted to look at our goodie box," said Robert. "Not much to see."

"We were looking for a blue notebook," I said, "a blue notebook belonging to a school girl, which seems to be missing, and we were wondering if maybe you had it."

"Why would we have it?"

"*Whether* you had it," I said, and there was a pretty good threat in my voice, too, because I don't take threats well, unless, of course, they come from the lieutenant, and then I take them very well. "But I guess if you had it you wouldn't hide it in the goodie box."

"I wouldn't *hide* it anywhere because I don't have it."

"The kids used to tease you," said Odd, falling back into that dreamy way he had when he was flashing back. "They'd call you Bony Pony, because you were so skinny, all skin and bones."

The chief looked for a moment as though someone had taken a ballpeen hammer to his heart. Robert suppressed a snigger, still not beyond the stage where he couldn't appreciate a good burn at someone else's expense.

"Come back to my office," said the chief to us. "Robert, put their prisoner in the lockup."

Knowing Houser was going back to where he gnawed open a vein, and seeing his reaction to same, made me want to get comfortable with the chief and spend some quality time. Who knew if Houser would draw any time in Spokane? He might as well draw a little here.

The chief shut the door behind us in his little office. We all sat down, the chief behind his desk. "I think it's time you tell me what's going on here," he said.

"I think you know what's going on here," said Odd. "That's why you've been following us, just like you dogged me when you were a little guy, Bony Pony, and I was Jeannie, the girl of your dreams."

This was a man who could hold his mud, anyone could tell, and had been doing same all of his days, but I saw before me a shaky mountain about to slide.

"I don't know how you know what you know," he said, "but I am a Christian, and I know we don't come back; we go to heaven or hell. Jeannie is an angel now. She was an angel here on earth, and now she's an angel in heaven."

"I'm a Christian too," I said, "a hard-kneed Catholic, but even the Pope leaves a door or two open, and now that I think about it, we salute a good miracle. You may be a God-fearing Christian, but your people not so long ago used to send their souls to trees and winds and eagles flying across the sky. Who's to say they were wrong? The angel has come home again, buddy, in the form of this big Swede. You see his big right hand? Well, Jeannie's gonna lift that hand and point the finger at someone. You were twelve years old. Whatever they could have done to you then, they can't ever do to you now. Get it off you, Chief, before you have to live all over again, and who're you gonna be then?"

Whatever unraveling he was in the middle of came back together again in an instant, in his anger. I don't know what lit him up worse, my accusing him of murder or my shaking his comfortable concept of heaven and hell.

"Me? You think I killed James and Jeannie. I worshipped her. I thought she was the finest thing nature ever made. I was twelve years old! All I wanted to do was be around her."

"You were jealous of James. He had her and you wanted her. Yes, you were twelve, crazy, no controls on yourself. You picked up the family shotgun—you knew where they would be that night—your folks thought you were snug in your little bed, but you were hiking up to that lovers' lane carrying your shotgun! James was not going to have her, was he!"

"I'm gonna knock you on your ass. I don't care if you are a woman!"

We were both on our feet, but forget about me backing down. "Who's holdin' you back, Tonto? Take your best shot."

Odd said in a soft voice, "He's not the one." I guess I heard him or I wouldn't be able to tell it now, but it was lost in the heat of facing down the chief. I wanted a killer, and quick, so I could get off this damn island and take my prisoner with me.

"You had a connection to Jeannie," I yelled at him, "a powerful one. Why didn't you tell us?"

"Why should I tell you anything?"

"James rolled down the window to you!" I yelled in his face. "Why wouldn't he? Bony Pony?"

"I cried for three days! You ever see an Indian cry? No one saw me either, you fuck!"

I was startled, I admit. Somehow I knew this man had said "fuck" maybe three times in his adult life and never in front of a woman, but he was right in front of me, six in-ches from my nose, calling me a fuck.

"He's not the one," Odd said, and before either of us could say anything else, we heard a frightened yell from Robert, "Chief! Chief, oh, shit! Oh, shit, shit, shit! Chief!"

We rushed to the adjoining door, threw it open. Houser was ricocheting off the walls and bars of his cell, splatter-ing blood everywhere. His face was dripping with it. The son-of-a-bitch was chomping on his last good wrist.

16

It was one in the morning by the time we got back to the Honeymoon Cottage, and I needed to sleep.

We rolled over the gravel, and in the quiet night, I thought we must be waking up half of Canada. We helped Houser out of the car. I hissed, "Asshole."

"You shouldn't have put me in that cell," he whined.

Both the chief and Odd had struggled to hold him down, while Robert was running around trying to find their first-aid kit. I remembered the half-full pint of Kessler's in the evidence box and grabbed that instead. I squeezed between the two men, cleared a field for Houser's bleeding wrist, and poured most of the cheap whiskey over his wound. The rest I poured into his mouth. Choking it down had a calming effect on the toothy creep.

"No, Robert shouldn't've took off your cuffs, da frick. What the hell was he thinking?"

Which was one of the questions, one of the several questions I hollered at Robert while we checked Houser's cleaned-up wound, which was ugly as rot but no more than superficial. Why in the hell did you take off the cuffs? I hollered at him. *How* in the hell did you take off the cuffs? They had keys, too, you know, he told me, quite defensively, and one of them fit our cuffs, so why shouldn't the poor guy be a little comfortable in the lock-up? He never did anything to Robert, after all.

Now our perv had both wrists bandaged up and I was fretting over a fresh round of fevers and puking.

"You will not get sick all over again," I said. "There is no place for you to get sick, and no one to take care of you if you do… so don't."

He looked up at me with a hang-dog face.

We pulled him up on the porch and opened the door. Stacey and her mother were asleep in the bed. Gwen's head lifted to watch us come inside, but the kid never did stir. Gone to dreamland.

The door locked from inside.

We made a pallet on the kitchen floor for Houser and laid him down. I cuffed his one hand to an exposed pipe and the other to some cabinetry. It was not the most comfortable position in which to try to get a night's sleep, but we were not going to take any chances on him cannibalizing himself again. If he were up to it and had the necessary dexterity, let him chew on an ankle. Da frick.

We turned out the lights and Odd and I undressed in the dark, down to our skivvies. I lay down on the davvy and pulled the bedspread over me. Odd pulled a blanket over himself on the rocking chair.

"I'm dead," I whispered.

"It's been a long day," said Odd.

"You know what we kinda lost sight of, in all the shit that's happened?"

"Ron," he said.

"Yeah, Ron. Who is he? Where is he? Is he on the island, even? How do we find him?"

"Maybe he'll find us, if he's still alive and on the island. We've made ourselves known."

"Odd..., how long can this go on? We've had our over-nighter, I've gone along with that, and, yeah, I'm convinced. You've been recycled, and for maybe the best of all reasons. But at some point soon we've got to deliver our prisoner... or call someone else to come get him and quit our jobs and just live here."

"You don't have to be involved. I told you."

"I've been wondering about that."

"It's not your thing, Quinn. You don't have to go through this with me."

I didn't, of course. I was fully capable of throwing the perv in the backseat and driving alone to Spokane. I knew I wouldn't, though.

"You and me don't have that much in common, Odd. After we're both cops, there's not much to say."

Which he didn't.

"So why is it," I asked, "we're here together? Why is it we always wind up buddying up?"

"Not always."

"Think about it."

"It's a small department."

"Who's your best friend, then, in the department?"

"In the department? I guess you are."

"Now, isn't that strange, because I would say the same thing, if somebody asked me."

"What's so strange about it?"

"You're a young guy; I'm a woman almost twenty years

older. I'm half a couple; you're a loner. I've never been to your place; you've never been to mine. You don't talk; I can't stop. You're a Protestant; I'm a Catholic."

"I don't see how that makes much difference."

"Maybe not, but I don't think we ever realized what friends we were 'til we came to this island. I'm wondering... if you had a life before, maybe I did too, and maybe we were buddies back then, all the way down the line. Now, this ain't coming from the head, it's coming from the gut, and lately I don't trust my visceral turmoils...."

"Your what?"

"I haven't trusted my gut for some time, but I'm lying here thinking, whatever you do, I gotta stay and do it with you. That's what I did before, and that's what I gotta do again... and again... and again. Whatever happens to you has to happen to me. That's why I have to stay, even though I don't want to. This thing...we do it together, we always have."

"What thing?" he asked.

"Die," I said. And then I fell asleep.

I could have slept a little longer. I would not have minded an hour or two more of sleep. Up to me, I would have slept the rest of the day away, but at seven in the morning there was a rap on the door. Not a Frank or Angie rap. A rap lacking politeness. A rap I recognized even though I was still half asleep, having perfected the technique myself. A cop's rap.

I sat up and gathered the bedspread around me. I was light in the head and may have been a little grogsick from last night's beers and martinis.

"I'll get it," said Odd. He took the few steps to the door in his boxer shorts and T-shirt, and I looked at his legs. He had great legs, lightly feathered with silky blond hair, and an oval birthmark on the back side of his right knee. I remembered having noticed it before, during volleyball, when I played in the back row and Odd was in the front.

He opened the door. I was right about the kind of knock.

A sheriff's deputy in a starched tan uniform, wearing bifocals in a set of Costco frames, stood on the porch. He was no spring chicken. He could have retired a couple years ago and opened up a security business, but he would have had to work too hard, and he would have had to leave the island. He looked like a guy taking it month by month now, any one of which might be a good time for his retirement dinner. He stayed lean, maybe abetted by the cigarettes he smoked. There was one in his shooting hand now.

Mother and child awoke, too, and they were sitting up in bed, the blanket pulled to their necks. Nothing from the tethered Houser, who might have died in his sleep, for all I knew. For all I cared.

"Yes?" said Odd.

The deputy didn't say anything at first. He was trying to process what he saw: two women in bed, another one on the davvy, a young guy in his skivvies.

"I'm Deputy Nascine, from the county," he said at last. "I run the substation on the island. Everything okay here?"

"Everything's fine here. Why?" said Odd.

"Some rumors going across the island," he said, leaning into our cottage, craning his neck for a better look.

"What kind of rumors?"

"You the cop from Spokane?"

"Was that the rumor?"

Odd, who got along with everybody, did not like this guy on sight, I could tell, and I knew they would be at it in another minute.

"He's one and I'm the other," I said. "What can we do for you so early in the morning?"

He looked at his watch. It wasn't early for him.

"My information was that you picked up a fugitive here on the island."

"That's right," I said, "on tribal land."

"A tribal fugitive?"

"Of course not. A white guy."

"That fugitive should have been put in my custody."

It looked like he'd step inside except for the fear that Odd might slam the door on his foot, because Odd was holding it that way.

"Whatever.... I guess if you busted him he woulda, but you didn't bust him. Anyway, he's with us now," I said, "like he's supposed to be."

"I think you miss my point, ma'am. I don't know what the man has done, what crimes he may have committed on the island. Rules say he's not your prisoner 'til I hand him over, and somebody's been hiding him from me."

"Well, that sounds serious as a kidney stone, deputy, but my information tells me the Indians, according to their constitution, can keep a honky for twenty-four hours before turning him over to his rightful masters. That's all that was done."

"The Indian constitution is for Indians. Your boy's not an Indian." He took the last drag on his cigarette and flipped it out to the driveway. He'd already said all that he wanted to say to me. He directed his attention to Odd. "Shining Pony and that excuse for a police station don't mean shit. I'd like to know who the fugitive is, what he done, and where he is right now."

"I'm here," called a frail voice from behind the counter, from the kitchen floor.

"Shaddup," said I.

"I'm gonna have to come in here," said the deputy.

"You're gonna have to stay outside," said Odd, taking a stronger grip on the door's edge.

Gwen and Stacey weren't saying anything. From the looks on their faces, they were waiting for the shootout.

"There are rumors that this prisoner's been mistreated," said the deputy.

"Not true," called Houser. "I'm my own worst enemy."

"Not while I'm around," I muttered.

"They've been nothing but considerate with me," Houser testified.

"You can turn him over now, or we can all hang fire while I call for backup."

Having given us our selections, the deputy leaned into the Honeymoon Cottage, bracing himself against the door frame with both hands, and waited for our answer.

Odd turned to me and said, "You know what? Let's turn him over and get him off our hands."

"I don't want to be turned over," moaned Houser. "I want to stay with you guys."

I saw something in Odd's eyes and played along. "Yeah, you're right," I said. "He's been a pain in the ass, and he'll probably beat the rap anyway... and we still have things to do on this island."

"What things?" asked the deputy.

"Oh, we got a project," said Odd.

"Didn't the rumors... your information... tell you about the project, Deputy? What's your first name, by the way?"

"Robert," he said.

"Jeez Louise, not another one," I said.

"What?" he said, distracted.

"This island is full of Roberts. Every other person is a Robert, I don't get it. Either that or infirm or fat or missing digits."

"Who are these two?" the deputy asked, nodding toward Stacey and her mother.

"Not Roberts," said Stacey.

I had to hand it to the sassy little cocksucker.

"It gets complicated, but they are part of the package here," I said. "Look, you want him, give us a minute to get dressed, we'll clean him up and hand him over to you and God bless, because he's kind of high maintenance."

"If he goes, I go," said Stacey.

"If she goes, I go," said Gwen. "I'm her mother."

"Definitely. There you are, deputy, three for the price of one."

Odd was fighting back his half-crooked smile.

Deputy Robert was taking in Stacey.

"I'm the 'victim'," Stacey volunteered. "Can you believe that? Victim of what?"

"We got nowhere else to go but here or with you, sir," said Gwen.

"Welcome to the lot of 'em, Deputy, with our compliments."

He pushed back from the doorframe, shook another cigarette out of a pack of Camels, and lit up. He looked again at his watch. "There's a 9:45 ferry to America. All of you, including you back there, you're gonna be on it. Get off my island and go back to Spokane."

"Fine," said Houser. "I want to. I don't like this island one bit."

Odd and I dummied up. We had already sold it; we weren't going to buy it back again.

The deputy went away acting as though he had carried out the law as he interpreted it. Big man, little island.

We slapped off a hi-five, like a couple of kids who had pulled a fast one on the face of authority, but we still had nowhere to go, nowhere but back to Spokane with our chewed-up fugitive. We still had Stacey and her mother waiting for Karl Gutshall to fix their Civic. We still had Connors back home doing God knows what with Esther. And we still had hot flashes by the bushels, at least one of us did. We still had Jeannie piggy-backing on the big

169

Swede. What we didn't have was whoever murdered her and her boyfriend, James Coyote.

My eyes dropped again to Odd's legs. I'd forgotten that a man can have such nice legs. He was standing in the open doorway watching the Sheriff's patrol car pull away. I focused in on that birthmark on the back of his knee, and I felt myself falling into it, the way you do when you lean out over a balcony from the sixteenth floor of a building that somebody's jumped off. I had already seen Odd pulled out of his body a couple of times in the past twenty-four hours, and now the same thing was happening to me. To tell you the truth, I half-enjoyed it, because I could have used a little vacation from that burning body.

I didn't know what yet, but suddenly that birthmark meant something to me.

"How long have you had that?" I asked.

"What?"

"That thing behind your knee."

"I was born with it. They call it a port wine mark."

Then it hit me. I flew out of my wrap, my heart pounding. I grabbed my jeans and rifled the pockets, but then I remembered Odd had driven last.

"Quinn? What the hell...."

I rifled his pockets and came up with the car keys. He asked me what I was doing but the adrenalin was pumping so hard I couldn't answer. I ran outside in my skivvies, doing a painful dance on the gravel. I got to the trunk of the car.

Frank was standing outside the main house, leaning on the porch rail, sucking up oxygen. He gave me a wave and a cheery "Good morning!"

Odd was standing on our porch now. I'm sure he was wondering from what new conniption he would now have to rescue me. Frank gave him a good-morning too, all smiles, probably believing we must finally be having a swell time in his little resort.

I opened the trunk and took my service baton from its holding ring. I rushed back to the porch. By this time, Stacey and her mother were standing in the open doorway, both in their skivvies, both probably worried that I was rushing in to beat the shit out of Houser.

Not a bad idea, but.

I stopped behind Odd and placed the baton along his port wine birthmark. It was a perfect fit.

"What are you doing?" he asked.

"Creeping myself out," said I, and I was.

I deputized Gwen.

Houser had not fallen sick, thank God, but he was not in the pink, either and I was damn sick of dragging him along. I made Gwen raise her hand and swear to a lot of stuff I made up on the spot with no authority whatsoever to administer same.

"Do you swear to enforce a distance between the prisoner and the victim sufficient enough to preclude any and all physical contact of any nature whatsoever?"

"I do," she swore solemnly.

"I do, too," said Stacey, though I was not fool enough

to swear that one to anything. I cuffed Houser's hands behind his back and gave the key to Gwen, pretty much shitcanning my career should she turn out to be irresponsible, and, da frick, she was already irresponsible or her daughter wouldn't be giving head to a guy more than twice her age.

Odd and I got back into yesterday's clothes. I didn't have a toothbrush, he didn't have that or a razor, but we pulled ourselves together as best we could while my new deputy brewed the coffee.

"Would you tell me where we're going?" he asked. We were using the bathroom together, having reached a new level of intimacy, I guess.

I envied him his short hair. All he had to do was wet it and run his fingers through it. My own was a mess and there wasn't a lot I could do with it. The Shenandoah solution, a *babuska*, was not available, so I pulled it back and tied it up. I looked like general hell, but I could care less.

"I'll tell you when we get there, I don't want to look like an idiot."

"A little late for that," he said, and I laughed.

Gwen handed us each a cup of coffee and we blew on it.

"Remember, sitting in James' four-by... how you knew something was wrong?

"Yeah..."

"Something was wrong."

"What?"

"That's what we're gonna find out, if we're lucky."

It was not easy going back to the tribal police headquarters and Chief Shining Pony. I was prepared to do a little groveling.

The second Robert was on duty and I gave him a dour good-morning, which he took warily and returned a grunt that I took as a greeting between enemies. He probably heard from the first Robert all about the ruckus last night, including the screaming match I had with his boss, the kind of match I never lose, by the way.

"Know where the chief is?" I asked.

"Mmm-hmm."

"Like, where?"

"In his office."

I belayed my usual cop's rap and tapped like a timid dormouse.

We went inside. To say the chief was a bigger man than I gave him credit for would not be accurate because I had always given him that credit. He understood that my shrewish behavior the previous night was borne on a cop's need for justice and her outrage that it had been denied for so long. I didn't tell him it was all multiplied by a factor of... whatever, by the hormonal desert maelstrom inside my body.

He reassured us that for the past thirty-three years he had wanted nothing more than to bring Jeannie's killer to justice. Apologies tendered and accepted, I asked him about the autopsy report.

"The county has all that; why didn't you go to them?"

"Because early this morning the county came to us. And ordered us out of Dodge."

"Nascine?"

"Yeah."

"He's an old hardass. When he was young, he was a young hardass."

"Yeah, well, I thought, I don't know, if I were Chief Shining Pony, I'd have copies."

Of course he did, but he was reluctant to show them, probably because to do same, in his mind, would add to Jeannie's humiliation.

"Quinn is onto something, Chief," said Odd. "I don't know what, but, please... let us see what you have."

He unhooked a ring of keys from his belt, found a small brass one, and opened a file drawer in his desk. He took out a folder and spread the pictures before us without looking at them himself. I could see why. She was naked on a slab, front and back, under bright florescent light. Above the neck, you wouldn't know she was human.

I glanced at the pictures then looked up at Odd. His expression as he studied them was unnervingly familiar to me. I tried to place it, and then it came to me: television news coverage of families returning to their homes after a vicious hurricane only to see a pile of trash. A look of benumbed detachment. He, like them, was looking at a former home now utterly destroyed by a force of evil.

While Odd was transfixed and the chief looked away, I scanned the report.

"There was semen in her," I said.

"Yes," said the chief. "They were sexually active."

"Without protection?"

"It was the sixties."

"Even in the sixties, high school girls did not want to get pregnant, and high school boys did not want to make them that way."

I quickly sorted the pictures, putting one atop the other, stacking them, until at the end there was one on top of all the others. It was the one I was looking for. I asked them to look.

She was lying on her stomach. I picked up a pencil from the desk and pointed to the back of Jeannie's knee. The bruise there was a perfect match to Odd's port wine birthmark.

For all of his life he had thought it was an inconspicuous flaw of the skin. Now, for the first time, he saw it had a purpose.

"Her head...," said the chief, and he faltered, "... well, you can see that.... The bruise on her leg was the only other mark on her. The murder book doesn't draw any conclusions."

"I'm gonna draw a conclusion of my own," I said. "That's a policeman's baton; that's what made that mark."

The chief looked at it more closely.

"I'll tell you something else," I said. "A cop is trained to pick up his spent shells. That's why there weren't any at the murder scene."

"What is Deputy Nascine's middle name?" Odd asked the chief.

"Bob Nascine? Not sure I know." He dug another file out of his desk drawer. "Should be here in the county roster ...."

He ran his finger down a list of names and stopped. "Oschel," he said. "Must be a family name."

"Robert Oschel Nascine," said I. "R.O.N."

"Ron," said Odd.

"She was out of the truck," I said. "She was running away. He hit her on the back of her knee with his baton, swung it hard, brought her down."

17

We counted backwards, and as hard as it was for the chief to imagine, Robert Nascine was only twenty-eight at the time of the murders. He had always seemed old to Seth Shining Pony.

Nascine came to the island from Bellingham where he had been a legendary high school basketball player, having led his team to a state championship in the days when five-ten was not short on the court. A few college recruiters came to call, but Nascine had already decided on a career, and, in those days, college was not a benefit to his choice: law enforcement. Everyone works for power, through money or position, but with a badge power is bestowed upon you. At least this is how the chief saw Nascine's motivation after years of first distant, then close, observation. For his own part, the badge was a burden, and the power it gave Seth Shining Pony was false and uncomfortable. Like now, for instance, upon wondering if a man known and feared for most of his life was responsible for the murder of the girl he idolized.

Scenes were now replaying for Odd, and it was powerful testimony, but from an eyewitness who would never be allowed to take the stand. It was evidence still incomplete at best and legally useless. He remembered Nascine, Deputy Bob, coming to Jeannie's school and making a scare presentation on the evils of marijuana.

"It was stupid. Even he couldn't pretend that he believed all that crap. All the kids giggled through most of it. But he was young, younger than the teachers, and handsome in his tan uniform. Some of the girls had serious crushes on him. Later, he came back."

When Deputy Bob returned to present a cautionary lesson on the consequences of drinking and driving, complete with gruesome audio and visual aids, a session for which he could find far more enthusiasm and to which the students responded with far more horror, Jeannie made her move. The deputy, she decided, would guide her through that awkward, embarrassing, and dangerous passage into womanhood. She knew her own power and was sure he would not refuse her.

"It happened in his cabin.... He was renting a bachelor's cabin, inland from Point Sinister..."

"I know the place," said Seth Shining Pony.

"They were toking on some weed he'd confiscated from somebody, and Jeannie got over her jitters, and everything he said was soothing... and so funny... and then her clothes were off... and it wasn't all that painful, and she was okay with looking at him after. For a few days, then, she thought she must be in love with him. She wrote his initials all over her notebook—since she was underage and he was a cop she was afraid to write his name—but her girlfriend caught her at it, and she had to tell her everything."

"Who was this girlfriend?" I asked. "What was her name?"

Odd shook his head. "I can see her... she's shorter than I, straight dark hair... dark complexion...."

"Tribal?" asked the chief.

"Yes! She's an Indian girl."

The one thing Jeannie hadn't anticipated was that Deputy Bob would fall in love with her. She was sure he was well experienced, and in fact he was, having had his reasonable share of high school beauties. But that was when he was in high school himself. Ten years later, all the cheering was over, and those girls disappeared into other lives. It was Jeannie who took dominion over his heart and mind.

"That's when the trouble started... the anger... the jealousy when Jeannie started going out with James," said Odd, and then he had to sit down. He was exhausted and could no longer follow the thread to its inevitable end.

"So Stacey was right," I said. "Jeannie had to tell somebody. She told her friend. You have to remember that friend's name, Odd."

He tried, but nothing was coming.

The chief remembered. He said, "Camilia Two Trees."

"Yes! It was Cammy! How could I forget her? We were best friends."

"Is she still around?" I asked the chief, "Is she still on the island?"

"Yes, she's still on the island. She's married to Bob Nascine."

That 9:45 ferry to "America," as Deputy Nascine had so quaintly put it, had once again chugged off without us. We were having breakfast at the cafe, where old man

Drinkwater was still holding down a stool at the counter and where all looked over their long stacks and bacon when we came in. They were looking at Odd. I recognized their expressions. Once in Spokane we had this transgender, girl to guy. He was built like a dumpster, with a hairy chest and a bushy beard and everyone who knew about the change would look at him and think: that man, that man used to be a woman.

The accommodating waitress, the young recovering alcoholic fry-cook, Drinkwater and his Indian chums, all the assorted palefaces, everybody knew by now, whether they believed it or not, that Jeannie, that fabled tragic beauty of thirty-three years ago, slain on our shores, was back, in the form of a big Swede cop from Spokane. And everyone knew why.

As we drank our coffee and waited for our pancakes, I leaned toward Odd and said, "Putting aside what we got waiting back in the Honeymoon Cottage, and what we got waiting back in Spokane, as I see it here, we got two possibilities."

"Both long shots, I'm guessing," he said.

"Camilia Two Trees Nascine knows everything and is so weary of the burden and so sick of a lifetime with Deputy Bob that she'll be willing to spill the beans, and he'll do us the great favor of eating his service revolver…."

"Or?"

"Or you do a face-off with Nascine. That is, Jeannie does a face-off with Nascine. Scare the wits out of him until he confesses."

"He doesn't scare easy."

"Hell he doesn't. He was scared when he came to the cottage this morning. He kept looking at you like at a ghost."

"Is that what I am, Quinn?"

Ghostly stuff was about him, for sure.

"No, you're flesh and bones, Kid, the physical part of you is."

"The physical part?"

"The other stuff..., I'm still sorting it out. It's like candles."

"What's like candles?"

I was looking for something that made sense, something that we could grasp.

"When a candle burns down, and you pass the flame to a new one, you get a new candle; but what about the flame? It's the same flame that used to be on the old candle, ain't? And that flame can pass from candle to candle, thousands of times, as many times as you have candles. Size of the candle doesn't matter, nor the color, whether it's a beautiful candle or a cheesy one.... One dying candle lights two new ones, ain't? Two from one. Ten from one."

That's how I finally did the math on this thing.

"I guess so."

"That's the way I'm sorting it out. That's something I can understand: a flame, passed from one candle to another, forever."

"That's nice, Quinn."

"Look, we're cops, okay? We're gathering evidence. I don't care where it's coming from if it nails the perp. We can work all that out later."

"Right."

"You're you and only you, but your light goes way back, and that last glow of light wants to make itself known. I mean, maybe that's the reason you were born, in Spokane...."

"I always hated Spokane."

"That don't matter. You were born there to become a cop to chase after Houser, the pedophile, to this island where the person you used to be lived and was murdered, so that person can face her murderer and bring him down."

"So what are you doing here?"

"Me? I got the mouth. Left to yourself, you wouldn't say boo."

"Maybe that candle lit both of us."

"Yeah, it's a pretty thought, Kid, but my light is sixteen years older than yours. If I did have a past life, it was probably as a peasant running away from some Cossack with a hard-on."

The door opened and once again everyone turned. It was Chief Shining Pony and under his arm was tucked a white leatherette yearbook, Class of 1967. He slid into the booth next to Odd and ordered a cup of coffee.

He put the yearbook on the table but didn't open it. Odd couldn't take his eyes off it.

"I put out the word," the chief said, "that you're still here doing something for me."

"So the heat's off as far as the county is concerned?" I said.

"You wish. Nascine always feels that if anybody's gonna do something for me it ought to be him. He'll still harrass you, but get yourself to tribal land if he does; that'll give you some protection."

"Nascine did it," I said. "I'll bet the farm on that. Ain't, Odd?"

"I don't know," he said.

"Even if he did," said the chief, "the only evidence we have is that bruise on Jeannie's leg that may or may not match a police baton. It might match the barrel of the shotgun."

"Wait a minute.... If Jeannie ran from the car... and Nascine brought her down with a baton to the back of the knee... and shot her... and then put her back in the car.... Why in the hell would he do that?... but that's not my point."

"What is your point?"

"My point is he came into physical contact with her when he picked her up and put her into the car again, which opens the possibility to his leaving on her what didn't exist back then... DNA."

"Nascine was the officer who discovered the bodies. He may have made the mistake of touching them."

"Nascine discovered the bodies?"

"Yeah."

"Of course he did," I said, disgusted.

It was amazing how little we knew about the case, and yet we had the possibility of knowing it all.

Odd wasn't even listening. He had opened the year-book.

I looked at the dedication page. Even upside-down I could see it was a blown-up snap of Jeannie and James, in a rain forest, covered with slickers, arms around each other, in a thick growth of ferns dripping with moisture.

"Anyhow," said the chief. "Jeannie's body was cremated. So was James', for that matter."

"Shit, piss, and corruption."

"I never met a woman like you, and I don't think that's a compliment."

Odd paged through the yearbook, and I could see in his face the recognition of old friends, the reliving of school activities from someone else's life. He stopped at one page and put his finger on a picture.

"Cammy!" he said, smiling.

I turned the book around and looked at the picture. Camilia Two Trees: Chorus, Stitch 'n Rip Club, Library Volunteer, Cheerleaders, Homecoming Princess. She had deep dark eyes and high cheek bones, a Mona Lisa smile.

"We were friends from the first grade," said Odd, "right up until...."

Together they must have made a formidable pair, the fair and the dark, beauties, both.

"I hope things turned out well for her," said Odd.

"You can see for yourself," said the chief. "She's helping out during the season at Rocketman's."

Rocketman's was at a T-intersection in the main peri-
meter road, set back in an acre of crushed rock where by
state law purchasers of fireworks were required to set off
same, and occasionally someone actually did, mostly as
a test before committing to a trunkload.

The stand itself was long and narrow and consisted
of a wide counter laden with pyrotech small fries, behind
which was a long wall in three tiers displaying the hard
stuff, in ascending order of fire power. After hours, it was
battened down by a series of hinged four-by-eight standard
plywood panels, hung during the day in an open position.
The whole thing was whitewashed, but stamped lumber
markings bled through.

Near the entrance was an old rusted pickup for sale,
with the bald spare tire mounted to the grille. The camper
shell that used to be on the pickup was on the ground at
the far end of the stand. It served as kitchen and break
room. A portable Honey Bucket toilet was set up at the
other end of the stand.

All signage was hand-lettered, including the large
Rocketman sign that sat on the roof of the stand, with
its logo of an Indian atop a blasting rocket. The others:
*NO SMOKING, MUST BE 16 OR OLDER, NO M-80S OR
LARGER WITHIN 150 FEET, VISA AND MASTERCARD
OK.*

Cheap plastic pennants in red, white, and blue were
festooned from the stand to outlying poles in the ground.
A string of Christmas lights ran the length of the stand for
nighttime sales.

We pulled onto the lot, drove over the crushed rock and up to the stand. We were the only car on the lot. Two teen-aged boys appeared from behind the counter, rising from their lawn chairs. They were bare-chested, wearing jeans that hung below their hips, revealing three inches of their boxer shorts. One was listening to rap music; the other was watching Jerry Springer on a jury-rigged battered black-and-white TV set. Goofy kids, both, but I would have killed for their hair, either one, glistening black, thick, and hanging down their backs in expertly crafted pigtails. My own had become brittle, dry, and thin. In moments of despair, I'd thought of shaving it all off and letting people think I had cancer, which, let's face it, is a tad more socially acceptable than menopause, if less forgiving at the end.

The boy at our end of the counter, the one listening to rap, which he hadn't bothered to turn down—Snoopy, Doopy, Dogg, Dogg, Gangsta, Bitchslap, Copkiller, Boyz, Noize—asked, "What can I get you, yo?"

I glanced over the exotic rainbow array of Chinese imports, everything from little hand-held poppers to diversionary concussion bombs, stuff I had never seen up close and had always regarded as slightly insane, just another way to split a tranquil night with ear-whacking discomfort. What possible satisfaction or joy could come by putting a match to these things? On the other hand, there are people who liked to be peed upon. No one can account for another one's pleasures.

"Is Cammy here?" I asked.

"Yeah, she's in the camper making tacos," said the kid. "Just go on in."

The camper door was open and we could see the back of a woman half as wide as the camper itself. Like the boys outside, she also had thick hair hanging down in pigtails. A few flies buzzed around her, but summer had not yet come with any real heat, so the bug population was sparse.

"Cammy?" said Odd, and it was a real question. More like, you can't be Cammy, my beautiful friend. If that's what Odd was thinking, what do you suppose Camilia was thinking, when she turned and saw a big Swede addressing her so familiarly.

What Rap Boy hadn't told me but would be explained to me some time later was that the tacos she was making were, more specifically, Navajo tacos. You take a bag of Frito corn chips, slit it along the long edge and puff it open like an envelope. Then you cover the chips with refried beans, grated cheddar, some salsa over the top. I couldn't wait to get home and try it myself. I was going to add diced kielbasa.

I wasn't sure Nascine had talked to her about Odd. I wasn't sure he ever talked to her at all; he might be that kind of husband. Indians, I was learning, unless they talked to you, didn't tell you much of anything, and even then sometimes left a lot to the imagination.

"Cammy," he said again, "is it you? Is it really you?"

"I'm sorry, do I know you?"

"When you were in fifth grade," said Odd, "you had this idea for a very exclusive club. You found the perfect cedar, and your idea was to build a treehouse in that cedar...."

Camilia took a step or two toward Odd. Her hands were trembling.

"It would be our clubhouse. You wanted to call it the Tree Top Club. But it was to be exclusive and secret so you said we should use just the initials and call it the T.T. Club, so that no one could guess where our clubhouse was. And I said, 'Think about it, Cammy... the T.T. Club? The Titty Club.' You were so embarrassed, and then we laughed and laughed, and that was the beginning and the end of the famous Titty Club."

Gripping the doorframe, she eased her bulk down to the step and sat there, benumbed, staring up at the big Swede.

"No one else ever knew about that," she said.

Earlier, the chief had asked me if I ever saw an Indian cry. I was seeing one now. Odd squatted down on the gravel before her and took her hand. He didn't say anything. She cried for a long time, then leaned forward and put her arms on Odd's shoulders and drew him to her. She pressed her face next to his.

"Jeannie," she wept, "Jeannie.... I'm so sorry...."

The rear of the camper was set back behind the fireworks stand, so the two kids working there could not see us, nor we them. At least there was that. I heard a car pull onto the lot. We were pretty well out of the sight of any customers, too, unless they decided to come back there and blow up a few Kamikazes. Unlikely as that might be,

I thought I'd better head it off anyway. Besides, I wanted to give Odd and Cammy a moment alone.

I slipped away without the two old girlfriends noticing.

"Hello, Sheriff," I said. Nascine was just getting out of his car.

"Deputy," he said.

"Right. I shot the Sheriff."

He stopped in his tracks and knitted up his brow.

"It's a song, Bob. 'I shot the Sheriff, but I did not shoot the Deputy.'"

I sang it loud, loud enough for Odd to hear and wonder what the hell. I circled Nascine and turned him around, so that I was looking past him, at the front end of the camper, waiting for Odd to appear. I wished he would.

"You're a real smart ass, ain't you?" Nascine said with a kind of free and easy venom, lighting up a Camel in defiance of a rather sensible rule against smoking near a fireworks stand.

"That is part of the profile, but I like to think I'm just misunderstood."

"Why are you still on the island?"

"Why else? Loading up on fireworks." I had missed a sign. *BEST DEALS.* "I hear Rocketman has the best deals."

I led Nascine over to the stand and started randomly selecting my arsenal from the back wall. The kids stacked them and tallied the price.

"Gimme an Ambush, an Atom Splitter, a Warp Speed...."

"Where's your prisoner?" asked the deputy.

"Offer's still open. You want him, you can have him, and the two females as well." To the kid, I said, "And I want a Texas Cyclone, a Dark Zone... a Golden Shower?"

"I don't name 'em," said the Springer fan, "I only sell 'em."

"Where's your partner?" asked Nascine.

"You took a real shine to him, didn't you?"

"Where is he?"

"People do take a shine to him. He's very popular. Every other month he gets named Officer of the Month; they give him that good parking place close to the door. The guy gives off a light, you know? I guess you could call it a glow, and everybody wants to kind of get within that glow. What a wonderful thing that is. I guess."

"What the fuck are you talkin' about?"

The f-word came much easier to this guy.

"My partner. You know, the way there's always one person in town that everyone is attracted to. The Golden Girl... or guy. He's an unusual guy. You never met a guy like him. I'd like for you to hang out together for a while, see what I mean."

"I'd like for you to get off the island."

"I can see that. I just don't know why. Or maybe I do."

"We don't like big city cops..."

"Big city? You ever been to Spokane?"

"... skirting our jurisdiction, cozying up to the Indians to get around dealing with the county."

"Which must be a pleasure, I'm sure. Next time."

"You are one smart-ass bitch, ain'tcha?"

"Now, you've crossed the line, Sheriff. Only my colleagues call me a bitch."

I really wanted to send a kick to his jewels, and I had a clear channel, as he was standing feet apart, arms folded across his chest.

"What else?" said the kid. They were in business here.

"What's the biggest thing you got?" I asked, still staring down the wiry deputy. "I want the most bang for my buck."

Both kids answered at the same time. "The Predator."

"Then give me two Predators."

"Where's my old lady, Calvin?" asked the deputy.

"Makin' tacos," Calvin told him.

"Yeah," I said, "We went back to see if we could buy some... Odd's still back there trying to strike a bargain... but here's the thing, they don't look like any tacos I ever saw before."

That's when Calvin gave me the recipe for Navajo tacos, and when Deputy Nascine ditched me and started walking, a little unsteadily in his cowboy boots across the crushed rock, to the camper.

The kids packed my fireworks into recycled grocery bags. The bill came to $285, which entitled me to a free Rocketman's T-shirt. I handed Calvin my Visa. No way would the lieutenant reimburse this one, and Connors was going to have a conniption when he saw the bill next month, but what could I do? Messing with people can cost you.

I dumped the stupid fireworks in the trunk of our Lumina. It was just then the yelling started.

18

I was driving again, but I didn't know where or what we would do next. We were cooling down. We had, after all, just assaulted a police officer, which is a serious offense everywhere in the world, unless it is committed by another police officer and it's personal. Those assaults rarely reach a court of law, and I was hoping this one would not be an exception.

Deputy Nascine had rounded that fireworks stand to find Odd on one knee, as though proposing, and Camilia Two Trees Nascine sitting on the camper step with her arms resting on his shoulders and in her eyes a look of such quiet joy that it had Nascine all but spitting. He had not seen that look since shortly after she had graduated from high school, when he married her. Now it offended him. Everything about her offended him. He started yelling, ugly words, accusations, insults. Odd stood up and backed away, and though he towered over Nascine, outweighed him by forty pounds, and had youth on his side, he appeared frightened… until Nascine backhanded his wife and called her a fat whore squaw. Then Odd grabbed the back of Nascine's collar, yanked him off her, and pinned him to the side of the camper, his forearm hard under Nascine's throat, the deputy high on his tippy-toes.

"Don't you ever hit her!" Odd hissed at his face.

I saw the deputy's arm flailing for his weapon, so I got to it first, unholstering the nine, popping the clip, clearing the chamber, all while Odd was choking the man. I threw the clip in one direction and tossed the nine under the camper. This was kind of serious too, disarming a peace officer. I would build my defense later, if I had to, but at the moment, I was more worried about Nascine shooting somebody, me maybe.

"You don't care about anything, do you?" Odd said to him, nose to nose.

If he expected an answer, he was going to have to let up on the guy's windpipe, because he was letting the deputy have just about enough air to stay conscious, and not for very long, either.

I put a hand on Odd's shoulder and said softly that we should go now, and with all deliberate speed. He released the deputy, who fell to his hands and knees, gasping. Those nicotine-coated lungs were very slow to fill. Camilia waved us back with the palm of her hand and indicated she could deal with all of this. So we motored.

"Where would you like to go, Odd?"

He didn't hear me. He was off somewhere, not in himself. We drove past the boatyard, past the *Northern Comfort*, on which James had earned his Ford pickup. I asked him again.

"Back to Jimmy Coyote's house," he said.

"Okay...," I waited for him to tell me why, or to tell me something, because I knew he had something to tell, but he sat silently. "Any particular reason?" Nothing. I waited a minute, then said, "Something happened back there, didn't it? I mean, besides you strong-arming the deputy."

He nodded.

He wasn't going to tell me. A cop is used to people not telling him everything. A cop has to fill in the spaces. I was doing that, beginning with the autopsy report. Inside of her was semen.

I took a detour to the Honeymoon Cottage. I wanted to check on that crowd to see what had gone wrong in our absence because surely everything had, but more than that I had to pee and I did not want to show up at the Coyotes' house asking to use the can.

Our three were sitting on the porch, just enjoying the nice day, Gwen sitting between the other two and keeping them at a safe distance, as she was sworn to do. I had a sudden and in some ways an alarming sense of well-being. I parked the car and we walked to the porch. I was trying to read their faces and I was drawing a blank, which could be a good thing.

"Welcome back, you two," said Gwen. "We were wondering if we'd been abandoned."

"Everything okay here?" I asked, on my way up the steps.

"Everything is hunky-dory."

I was passing them on my way into the cottage and to the bathroom with what was by now was an urgent need, when Gwen added, "Your lieutenant called from Spokane."

Oh, shit. Not a good thing, not nearly. I stopped, came back out onto the porch.

"Who gave you the message?" I asked, cautiously, hopefully.

"Oh, I took the call."

All hope gone, caution useless. "You took the call?"

"Angie yelled there was a phone call, so I went and took it."

"Don't worry about us," said Stacey. "We didn't do anything while she was gone. Hardly anything."

"You took the call?" I said again, and tried to get Odd's eyes, but who knew where he was? "You spoke to the lieutenant?"

"Don't worry, I played it cool," she said.

"Tell me what he said, and tell me what you said." My voice had the calm of death.

"He said where's his officers, and I said which one, and he said either one, and I said they were off, and he said where, and I said both off trying to solve the murder of the young guy—I forgot your name, I'm sorry—the young guy who used to be the young girl who was actually the one murdered but this was in a previous life."

"You said all that?"

"Was it supposed to be a secret?"

"Go on," I said, seeing my career thrown out with yesterday's coffee grounds. You play it careful your whole life and then something runs over you like you weren't even there.

"Well, he asked what kind of shape the prisoner was in, and I said it looked like pretty good shape 'cause he's right over there on the porch of the Honeymoon Cottage, and he said, 'What?'"

"He said what?"

"He said, 'What?' He was a little surprised."

I couldn't hold it in any longer. I was doing the wee-wee dance.

"Don't anybody say another word! Don't anybody move an inch! Not until I come back from the bathroom."

"Your Royal Highness...," said the brat.

"Not a word!"

What control can you hold over a situation when your back teeth are swimming? I made it to the bathroom, did my thing, and went into one of those hot flashes where I was sure my very duppa would ignite the toilet paper and I would go up in smoke.

I stripped off my clothes and jumped into the shower, setting the lever full right. This place, like the rest of the island, was on a well, and that deep ground water came out cold as ice picks. A minute of that did the trick. I toweled off, got my clothes back on, and went skidding back to the porch.

"The lieutenant was 'a little surprised,'" I prompted. "Don't tell me he was a little surprised; tell me what he said, and tell me what you said."

"I already told you. He said, 'What?' Surprised, like."

"And what did you say?"

"I told him not to worry because 'The Prisoner' was under house arrest, under guard."

"Did you, and this is very important, did you tell him Stacey was here, too?"

"Of course not. I told you I played it cool."

"Did he ask who you were?"

"Oh, yes, he wanted to know who I was."

"And did you tell him?"

"Yes...."

My hands were going for her throat. She saved her own life when she added, "I told him I was the deputy."

"Did he ask for your name?"

"No, he seemed satisfied."

"You told him you were a deputy, and he seemed satisfied?"

"Normally, it's not this hard for me to communicate with people, even if I do stand all day with a sign in my hand. People normally seem to understand me when I talk to them."

"The lieutenant was satisfied, okay. What did he say?"

"He said good-bye."

"Did he say anything else? Before he hung up?"

"Yes.... One other thing."

"I want the exact words."

She took a moment, either reluctant to repeat it or careful to make sure she had it verbatim. "He said, tell those two nimrods to get their asses home with the prisoner."

I paced the porch, talking to myself now. "This could be okay.... This might still work out... prioritize...:" But when I tried to get my priorities right in my head, Jeannie's murder and that prick Nascine kept coming out in the first position, in spite of myself. The lieutenant, however, must not call again and find us still here, and I knew Nascine was not going to take his roughing up without some form of retaliation. And if he believed what his wife was sure to tell him, that her long-gone girlfriend was back, it might be enough to rattle him into something quite desperate.

We had to get out of the Honeymoon Cottage. We were legally stuck with Houser, but we had to get rid of the other two and make ourselves a moving target, preferably on soil sovereign to the Shalish Indian Tribe.

"Odd? Odd, you still want to see the Coyotes?"

"Yes," he said. "We have to."

"Good. Let's do that. Okay, girls, pack up, we're checking out."

We were back in our uniforms, our weapons and gear strapped back on our hips.

Frank and Angie were sorry to see us go and a bit put out by our staying past the check-out time, which complicated their scheduling and clean-up. They hoped we had a good time and that we would come again. I had no energy left for convincing them we were not on vacation, not a family, not even friends.

Stacey and her mom would keep us in enemy territory just until we could drop them at Karl Gutshall's garage. Then we would go on to the Coyotes, for reasons still unknown to me.

I was driving again. It gave an outlet to my nervous energy, and I couldn't trust Odd to be in the same reality as the rest of us. We pulled up to the open bay and Karl came out from under their Honda Civic in his coveralls and his complementary cap.

He leaned into Odd's open window and said, "Afternoon."

"Karl," I said, "they're gonna wait here for their car, if that's okay with you."

"Okay with me, but they might have to wait some time."

"How long?"

"A week... two."

My heart dropped.

"The transmission needs a complete rebuild and finding the gears is gonna take a while, even if you're willing to go new, and I would recommend against that. I can always find used parts somewheres, but it takes time."

"Mr. Gutshall," said Gwen, "how much will this repair cost?"

"Oh, you're looking at about eighteen-hundred dollars."

Houser apparently wanted to analyze this because he jumped in and asked, "How much is the car worth?"

"Less than that," Gutshall admitted, which turned the whole thing into a no-brainer.

The lieutenant had said that Stacey and her mother were not our problem. Why could I not listen to him even in that? Why could I not just drop them by the side of the road? Odd was no help. Since beating up on Nascine he had gone all but autistic on me.

I sat with both hands on the wheel, hoping not to explode and torch us all, while Gwen signed over her title, which she always carried in her purse, expecting some day to need it at hand, and that day was now.

She bought her cars off a fella she used to date and she was sure he could find another for her and arrange an easy payment plan. I must admit I was impressed with her quiet acceptance of catastrophe. One day she had her own ride, the next day we were it, and that's the way it goes. Lucky for them, she said, that out on this island in the middle of nowhere they would run into nice people from home, us.

Odd seemed to wake from a slumber. He turned to Karl and said his name, almost plaintively. Karl gave him his full attention, as though he'd been hypnotized with one word.

"Karl," said Odd, "we're going to the Coyotes. Could you please come with us?"

Now, I didn't know why we were going to the Coyotes in the first place, and I sure didn't know why we would want to bring along Karl Gutshall, and since the Coyotes believed he killed their son, I could not for a moment imagine that Karl would ever want to go there, but guess what?

He said, "Well, I was about to close up anyhow. I only do half a day, Saturdays."

"And could you bring some tools?" asked Odd.

We were on our way again, not only with the two warm bodies I didn't expect to be carrying, but with a third extra that raised the ride to the level of low comedy. Karl took Gwen's place and she squeezed upon his lap, which did not seem to inconvenience her one bit. His bag of tools were in the trunk, along with my two grocery bags full of fireworks, and all the luggage.

We were still a mile or two shy of Indian Territory when we had to stop again. Walking slowly but as fast as she could was Cammy Nascine, her great buttocks rolling with each labored step. She was holding something, pressing it against her bosom. Her face was bruised and one eye blackened. She was drenched with sweat.

I pulled over and Odd was out in an instant, trying to comfort her. Nascine, of course, had inflicted the damage. Then, everyone was out of the car. We all clustered around Cammy.

Gwen said, "Honey, I've been there. Some men…, well, it's all they have left. You don't want to be around them, then."

"Mother, this isn't about you," whined Stacey.

"No, young lady, it isn't. It's about you. Look, listen, and learn."

"When he left he was in a hurry," said Cammy, about Nascine. "I went to his workshop. He had it hidden behind a fishing pole rack, but I always knew it was there. It's all I wanted to take with me."

It was Jeannie's secret notebook, just as Odd had described it. A blue spiral notebook with stick-ons of the Beatles and psychedelic flowers, and the name Jeannie on the cover in silver ink and on the bottom printed in block letters: *PRIVATE PROPERTY!!!!* Cammy handed it to Odd, returning it after all these years to its rightful owner, sort of.

"He found it back then, when they searched Jeannie's room, and he stole it out of evidence, and he kept it ever since. He couldn't bring himself to destroy it, because to him it was proof that Jeannie once loved him, and as old as the old fool is, he had to hold on to that. Why do you think he married me? I was the next best thing. Why did he stay with me? 'Cause I knew.'"

"Knew what?" I asked.

"That for one moment in time, Jeannie might have loved him."

"Did he kill her?"

"I can't ask myself that question."

"I asked it."

"Leave it," said Odd, turning my own words back on me. "Get into the car, Cammy."

She got into the back seat, leaving room for only one additional person of any size. We were going to have to jettison somebody, and it wasn't going to be me, not with Nascine on the prowl. Odd got behind the wheel, the rest of us apparently expendable.

"Okay," I said, taking charge. "Karl, you're going to have to wait here."

"No," said Odd, "we need Karl."

"Why?"

"He's got to get the pickup running again."

Huh? It was either discuss it and run the risk of getting busted by the county or making some kind of forward progress. I put Karl in the back next to Cammy, and I put Houser on Karl's lap, over his protests, of course.

Stacey and her mom, who were not our problem, who were never our problem, I abandoned on the side of the road and could care less if I cared at all, which I didn't.

Gwen, who probably wished she were dead anyway, accepted her fate, but Stacey went off on a rant, describing the nature of the lawsuit which would go into the multi-millions should anything happen to either one of them as a result of my callous disregard for their safety. We left them in the dust.

Old man Drinkwater was sitting on the porch with the Coyotes. They were not surprised to see us. It seemed they were waiting for us. If not for us, then for something, because Deputy Nascine had already been there.

And why?

"He wanted to make an offer on James's old pickup," said Drinkwater.

"Nascine wanted to buy the truck?" I asked. "After thirty-three years?"

"And at a pretty good price, too."

I looked at the Coyotes, wondering.

"We didn't sell it," said Mr. Coyote.

"When the deputy saw he wasn't gonna be able to buy the four-by, he started up saying how he could confiscate it, by law. He demanded to know where it was. He was pretty hot about it."

"Did he confiscate it?" Odd asked, worried.

"I ain't there yet," said Drinkwater.

"Then where are you?" said I.

"Deputy was wanting to know where it was. To keep my friends from having to lie, I said it was towed away to the Tribal Headquarters garage, long ago these many years now."

"Which was a lie," I pointed out.

"The Coyotes are respected for their honesty. I am respected for my lies."

"Sorry. Go on."

"I was one step ahead of him. I knew he would want to know why the truck was at Tribal Headquarters garage."

"Did he?"

"He did. I told him for the rite of purification."

"Is there such a thing?"

"No, but he does not know that. Here is the funny thing."

"It was very funny," said Mr. Coyote, dead-pan.

"What?" I asked

"The Tribal Headquarters," said Drinkwater, "don't have no garage, never did."

No one on the porch cracked a smile, though I could sense all three of them thought it was hilarious.

"So the skinny deputy went off mad," Drinkwater continued, "and we have been sitting here waiting to see who showed up next. Cammy, did your husband do that to you?"

Cammy went up onto the porch and sat down with them and didn't say a word, but apparently she didn't have to. Mrs. Coyote said, "You can live with us now."

Cammy nodded, and that quick a domicile was changed.

No similiar offer was tendered to Houser, who by now was also sitting on their porch and, in fact, was manacled to it.

We untarped the truck and once again pushed it out of the shed. Karl got to work. The rubber was fine, after being pumped back up to forty psi. He traded off the dead battery with the Coyotes' own pickup, along with the spark plugs. What else he did I paid no attention to, pulling Odd away and trying to get out of him just why he wanted to get that old truck running again.

He acted as though I should know. Da frick. About the time I got him focused enough to tell me, we heard wheels on the gravel and saw an official car. At first I thought it had to be Nascine coming back, and my hand fell upon the butt of my weapon, but it was Chief Shining Pony and out of his car spilled Stacey and her mom.

Odd was pleased to see them, though I could care less. They were not my problem, not, that is, until Stacey rushed to Houser, cooing and kissing and assuring herself of his well-being. By now, it seemed, I was the only one outraged by this continual flaunting of a felony. Everyone else seemed to be accepting of nature taking its own course, no matter how inappropriate.

I grabbed her by the hair and yanked her off him. Her hands went out to him as I pulled her away. I was sweating and furious. I noticed Odd watching our little scuffle with cool disinterest and then with a broad warm smile. At long last these illicit... illegal... lovers had a purpose in his dreamlike mission, and he told us what it was.

No way, I said. Never. Indefensible. The chief agreed with me, though he pointed out he had no jurisdiction. Cammy agreed with me. Karl agreed with me. Gwen, out of her diminishing shreds of motherly concern, agreed with me. The three old Indians sat impassively on the porch. Houser and Stacey were all for it.

19

The plan was highly suspect. It was short-sighted, it was underboard. It was irresponsible, unprofessional, and insupportable. It bordered on the irrational, the other-worldly, the insane. Worst of all, it was extremely dangerous, and it probably wouldn't work anyway. I bought into it.

Just before nightfall, when the rain returned, Houser and Stacey made their pass through town in Jimmy's four-by, just a couple of kids in love. Houser was wearing my sweatshirt, the hood pulled over his head, and Stacey had on Odd's black windbreaker, so that her blonde hair fell over its collar in sharp contrast. The rain created a muddy film on the windshield and Houser had to slow down and find the wipers switch. Those bewildered people who were afoot stopped in the rain and watched them drive by.

Houser followed his directions to Point Despair, put it into four-wheel drive, and plowed through the mud. They trilled wheeeeeee! and fishtailed to a particular spot drawn on a piece of paper by Odd. He backed up the truck and turned off the ignition.

Now that they were alone, on their own, unshackled, and free to do whatever inspired them, they kissed. The rain fell and they kissed. The hours passed and they kissed. They tried to play the radio but it was broken, so they kissed without accompaniment and without me saying they could not do same. I suspect they fondled, too, as well as other inappropriate behavior. Da frick.

Midnight came and the rain stopped. A light fog drifted in from the Sound. Houser and Stacey were kissed out and fighting against sleep.

Now, the butt end of a Camel drops from the open door of a Sheriff's unit, hisses, and dies in the mud. A fresh one replaces it in the mouth of the 61-year-old deputy who swings his legs to the outside and pulls on his clamming boots. He takes off his slicker and reaches for the shotgun.

Pausing for a moment, he listens. Only the non-sound that fog makes that you think you can hear. He crooks one arm around the shotgun and lights another Camel. He walks up the hill.

It is one thing for a handful of Indians to see the same ghosts, even for a handful of whites to get swept up in their vision, but it is another thing for an experienced lawman to believe that Jeannie and Jimmy ride again, as was reported, even though this very thing has happened so many times in his restless dreams. Jimmy in a hooded sweatshirt, Jeannie a sunburst of yellow hair.

Now, the cigarette hangs stuck to his lips, and he stands nonplused. It is not a truck just like Jimmy's—it *is* Jimmy's truck, backed into the same spot, and this wet night no different really from that one, except that he is old now. His breath comes hard.

He walks an arc over rutted tracks and goes into a stand of trees, as before. He squats for a moment, the shotgun level across his legs, and he listens, as before, and, as before, he hears: murmurs, the mouth music of a young girl, a sleepy giggle, filling him with desire and despair.

Only several steps separate him from the driver's side. As he takes the steps the window slowly rolls down. He is not only seen and noted; he is recognized.

The hooded head is turned slightly toward Jeannie and blocks part of her face. Will no one say anything, this time? He feels no rage this time. Only a blackness in his heart and a thing he must redo. He pumps a shell into the chamber.

But a high-pitched whistle shrieks above his head and he crouches involuntarily and looks above: a golden shower of sparks bouncing light off the fog. He is eye-level with the window. They look at him as though he were the ghost, and he himself is sure of nothing now.

He rises to his full height. He brings up the shotgun and now the air around him, on all sides, is hammered: explosions on all four sides. He feels compressed, unable to breathe freely. The next explosion is his own, fired into the cab of the truck. But no one is inside. The passenger door is open. He looks for them. They are running into the trees, hand in hand, screaming, either in terror or delight, or both. He pumps again and shoots over the hood of the truck, but they have disappeared.

The sky lights up again, cracking, chattering, exploding. He is blinded by the light, deafened by the din. He looks for his spent shells.

In a flash of light, he sees the Spokane cop, in the clearing, in uniform, just standing there, watching him, studying him. This is the one the Indians say is the reincarnation of Jeannie. He pumps another shell into the chamber and puts the shotgun to his shoulder.

It was an outrageous plan, off-the-wall, according to no book, as if we had ever read any of those books. We were not tacticians, not detectives nor sting operatives. What we were was: "See the man, see the woman, domestic dispute at, taillight out, expired plates, rear door ajar at, dead dog at...."

It was the kind of plan behind which, if done well, someone was likely to be shot. Engineered by Odd, who was at best in a dream state, it was the kind of plan in which everyone would get shot.

Odd stood there in the clearing, arms akimbo, under the lights and the pounding of the ingeniously platformed fireworks set up by Calvin and Rap Boy, the Indian pyrotechnos, staring down the killer of his former self, daring him to do it again, on into eternity, if it worked out that way, because that's as good a hell as any.

Having helped with lighting the fuses, with perfect timing, I must say, I hunkered down behind a tree and now had three choices: shoot Nascine (not an option, really; I'm a terrible shot), watch my partner bite it, or take the running dive and try to knock Odd out of the pellet pattern. I took the dive, ready for anything but where I would land.

Korea. In the dead of winter.

Chosin Reservoir.

A place I had never heard of, yet now was suddenly as well-observed as an ancient curse.

It was cold enough to freeze the blood of the corpses we were using as barricades. There were four of us left alive: Gertz, Fischer, my boyhood pal Tommy Hill, and me,

Clarence Washington. Tommy and I had played basketball together at Overbrook High, Philadelphia. After graduation we went to work on the same day at the same plant, Standard Pressed Steel. Now we were U.S. Marines, making a stand, surrounded by our frozen dead, trying to knock out a sniper's nest, so that at best we could go somewhere else to get killed.

The Chinese had 120,000 men; we had 15,000.

A wave of them came at us. We would be overrun. We shot from the hip.

Gertz went down and a second later Fischer's face exploded.

"Good bye," said Tommy.

"I love you," said I.

I took a bayonet in the arm, reached around for my fallen weapon and came up with a camp shovel. I sliced half-way through the neck of the soldier behind the bayonet and drove the shovel into the chest of another. I pushed Tommy away from one thrust, only to throw him into the path of another. Then, all the air I had went out through my chest at the point of the bayonet that went into my back, and that's the last I knew of it until this very moment, this moment of flying through the air, heart pounding, to knock Odd away from the shot Nascine took at him.

We lay in the mud, looking at each other, Tommy, Odd, Tommy, Odd.... Quinn, Clarence, Quinn, Clarence.

"My God," he said, "we've always been together!"

"You were there, just now?"

"Korea."

We held each other, now on the wet American soil, pinned down again, this time by Nascine, who stood over us and pumped a fresh shell into the chamber. Honestly, neither one of us cared. He didn't matter anymore.

The Deputy put the shotgun to his shoulder.

"Why did you suddenly want to buy the truck?" I asked. "Just curious."

"You don't know?" he asked.

"I do," said Odd. "When you killed Jimmy, Jeannie tried to run. You chased her and brought her down with a baton blow, back of her knee. You were going to finish her off right there, right here, in the mud, but the look of fear in her face aroused the real monster in you, the one that has always lived there. You dragged her to the back of the truck, out of the rain, on the mover's pad Jimmy had spread out back there, and you raped her. You raped her with the boy she loved sitting in the cab, where she could see him, with his head blown off. Then you sat her next to him, and by that time she welcomed the shot that you fired. The only hard evidence, the notebook, you stole, so you had no worries. Until I came along, because I would know, wouldn't I? And in the years that have passed, DNA would be discovered, and the back of that truck was still loaded with your DNA, your semen, and no way to explain it."

"Guess what?" he said. "I'm gettin' a little aroused right now. But, c'mon, you can tell me, how do you know all that?"

"You don't know?" said Odd, giving his own words back to him.

"That shit about you being Jeannie, reincarnated? No, that don't fly."

"Jeannie talked herself into loving you, for about two minutes. It was how she tried to deal with her own shame... and disgust."

"Disgust?"

"Disgust and confusion. It was her first time. She was young and inexperienced. She didn't understand why a grown man would cry like a baby after an orgasm."

If I could have touched Nascine with a stick at that moment, he would have cracked into a thousand little pieces. But I was still in the mud with Odd, watching the Deputy's finger on the trigger.

"Good-bye," said Odd.

"I love you," said I.

Now, from the trees behind us, a sharp crack, and Nascine yanked back as though on a string, right out of one of his clamming boots.

Odd and I disembraced each other.

Chief Shining Pony walked out of the trees behind us, cradling a 30-30 carbine. He didn't ask after our well-being, and he didn't check out Nascine. He didn't have to. Some deaths have a way of leaving no doubt. What he did say, with an economy I appreciated, was, "That's that."

"Thought you didn't want any part of this," I said.

"Only this part."

I sat where I was and watched Nascine. He lay motionless, his mouth open to the fog, his body slowly settling into the mud. What now, I wondered. Clarity gone, all linkage broken, attachments let go, fluids drying, skin cooling. Not a life led well; an existence gone monstrous. Was it over? All that was over, I realized, was that nicotine-stained body lying in the mud. The true Nascine was moving on. Would he get it right this time, would he find compassion and identification with his fellow human beings? Would he even be a human being, or did he lose that blessing? Would I know him when I saw him again, or should I always be aware that he could be anybody?

I arose from the mud with a sense of calm and well-being. My felon and his willing victim were probably halfway to Canada. I could care less.

20

We hit I-90 East just as dawn was cracking, or as is the case in Seattle, insinuating itself. This time, Odd was driving. One of his tapes was on. "Driving-into-Dawn Music."

Against all my predictions, Houser and Stacey had done the right thing, finding their way to Tribal Headquarters and calling 911. So we were taking Houser back after all and our careers, at least for now, were still intact. Of course, we had Stacey and her mother, too, all in the cage in the back, their luggage filling our trunk, with our muddy uniforms. We were back in our casual civvies.

When we went back to the Coyotes and woke everybody up, Odd was the one who told them who had killed their son, so long ago. They took the info and just nodded. Cammy, the newly widowed, had a tearful moment and closed the book on a lifetime of regret. Chief Shining Pony had stayed behind to deal with the minutia of a violent death and the closing of a 33-year-old murder case.

Odd took an hour and went off alone to talk to the woman who used to be his mother in another life. Whatever happened there I don't know and Odd never said.

We had a lot to talk about, the five of us, and the rehash carried us all the way to Ellensberg. His underaged girl-friend was concerned about what would happen to Houser now.

"Can't you put in a good word for him? He did help you."

"Sure," I said, "we'll say that he was very helpful."

"You're not just saying that?" asked Stacey, ever distrustful of me.

"Credit where credit's due. He may be a disgusting short-eyes, but he did help catch a killer, and he didn't give us any trouble, unless you count chewing up on his wrists."

"I went a little out of control," said Houser.

I chuckled at the understatement.

"You know wheat else?" said the perv.

"What else?"

"We forgot all about my car."

"Wha...?"

"My car. They still have it. I think it's still in the casino parking lot."

Now Odd chuckled.

"We've been stuffin' all these warm bodies into one small vehicle," I said, feeling pretty stupid, "when all along we had another set of wheels."

Shouldn't we go back and get it?"

"No way."

"But...."

His rig could rust away on that weird-ass island for all I cared. It wasn't my problem.

"I'm still making payments on it," he whined.

"So by the time you get out," I said, "it'll be paid for, 'cause you're gonna do some time, dude."

"How much?"

"Don't know. Make a deal. Go for... for digital penetration. How much can a finger-fuck be worth?"

"Now who's being disgusting?" said Stacey.

"Besides, it's not true," said Houser. "We wouldn't do that."

"Then make a deal for the least of what you did do. I could care."

I could. I was colossally disinterested in the outcome of Houser's case, or in their peculiar sex life, or in my own peculiar sex life or lack of same. There is more under the heavens.

By Moses Lake, Stacey and Houser had each fallen asleep against one of Gwen's shoulders. Gwen, propped up on each side, her head back, fell asleep as well.

We waited until then to broach the subject of our mutual past, so to speak.

"Have you ever even been in Philadelphia?" I asked him.

"Not in my life. You?"

"A few times. With the old man, to see the Phillies play. Once with some girlfriends to see a Little Richard concert. It was the big city to me, pretty intimidating."

Yet now, driving across the Washington prairie, we could both see our old neighborhood, our school, the sights and sounds of Standard Pressed Steel where we worked together before the war. We could see Paris Island and Marine boot camp. And we could see the battle of Chosin Reservoir, at least from our limited perspective, and we could feel the bone-breaking cold and finally the wounds that killed us both.

"It explains why I was always drawn to you," he said, and added quickly, "as a friend. Okay, there were a couple hot dreams...."

"I'm gonna slap you upside the head."

"And I always knew you had a special feeling for me."

"Not that special," I said.

I wondered, though, at what point true friends hook up, how far back does the connection extend? What war, what struggle, what century? I wondered if Odd and I always carried weapons, back through the ages? Were we made to be centurions and soldiers?

The battle of Chosin Reservoir took place in November, 1950. (I had to look it up on the internet.) I was born January 11, 1951, the same day as Jeannie Olson, but a continent apart. She was killed in April, 1967. Odd was born the next month, just before Memorial Day.

In April of 1967, it was all I could do to stay in school. I was two months away from graduating but I wanted to drop out and go somewhere. At the time I thought it was just my eagerness to see a wider world. I lived in the coal regions, after all, and almost all the kids were leaving. But with me it wasn't really eagerness; it was some kind of anxiety. Something was pulling me westward. I was born, or reborn, in Pennsylvania, Jeannie in Washington, and in 1967 it was time for us to link up again… only that wasn't going to happen this time because Nascine intervened and murdered Jeannie.

I told all this to Odd. "Then you would be reborn in Spokane. I would meet Connors in California, and we would go back to his hometown, and somehow you and I would wind up on the same police force. Woi Yesus."

We realized that all of that, all that we knew, was nothing compared to all the questions we would never have answered.

I don't know to this day if Odd ever told another soul, but I did. I told the story, first to Connors, then to a select few others. It's an entertaining story, in its way, whether believed or not, and, frankly, it is a little hard to believe. I have told it here for the last time. I could care less who believes what.

In the backseat, behind the cage, the felon and his lover and her mother slept on. I kept Odd awake, until I saw he didn't need me to do that. We fell silent for a long stretch of road, until we hit the city limits.

"Spokane, Washington," said Odd.

"Home," said I.

"I never much liked it here."

"Me neither," said I. "But here we are."

"We oughta get out of this place, move away, start over in another place."

"We?"

"You and me. We belong together."

"No, let's live it out here. There's always after."

"There is no new consciousness born, and no consciousness is ever destroyed. All consciousness resurfaces somehow. That's why we continue to go from life to life, all of us, the same beings, from the limitless beginning of time... every sentient being has been your mother."

Rimpoche Nawang Gehlek